# THE SECRET HERO

Businesswoman Marissa Boyd is completely in love with her favourite fictional character, daring Private Investigator Brett Morgan of the Ace Detective Agency. He is her secret hero and ideal partner . . . until she meets best-selling crime-writer Jonathan Gray. Unaware of Jonathan's real identity as Brett's creator, Marissa begins to replace dreams with reality. But Jonathan already has plans to marry the unscrupulous Nerina — who has her own agenda concerning Marissa's future and her new business venture . . .

BEVERLEY WINTER

# THE SECRET HERO

*Complete and Unabridged*

LINFORD
*Leicester*

First published in Great Britain in 2007

First Linford Edition
published 2008

British Library CIP Data

Winter, Beverley
  The secret hero.—Large print ed.—
Linford romance library
1. Love stories
2. Large type books
I. Title
823.9'2 [F]

ISBN 978–1–84782–379–3

Published by
F. A. Thorpe (Publishing)
Anstey, Leicestershire

Set by Words & Graphics Ltd.
Anstey, Leicestershire
Printed and bound in Great Britain by
T. J. International Ltd., Padstow, Cornwall

This book is printed on acid-free paper

# 1

Mrs Rose Nibela clicked her tongue in disgust as she tapped on the study door. Deftly balancing the tea tray in one hand, she turned the brass handle and marched resolutely into the room.

'Your tea, Professor Gray,' she announced firmly.

He hadn't eaten a thing all day and it was now four o'clock in the afternoon; not that he'd thank her for reminding him. He would be in one of his *trances* again.

The large man seated at the desk was indeed staring in front of him, his brow creased in fierce concentration. Mrs Nibela sighed. At these times nothing was real but the imaginary world he was creating inside his head.

'I'll leave it on the desk, sir,' she told him with a despairing glance at the papers and books scattered about its surface. How was she expected to dust and clean, let alone find a place for unimportant things like trays of tea?

Her boss started. 'What . . . ?'

'Your tea,' she repeated patiently. 'There's a nice fruit scone, too.'

He thrust a tanned hand through his much-raked dark hair so that it stood untidily on end, rather like one of her kitchen mops. She noted in concern that he'd forgotten to shave too; the undoubted result of a preoccupation with one of those complicated plots he was always weaving.

A much published author, Professor Gray had recently resigned from the English department at the university and was hurling himself into his writing with such ferocity that even his housekeeper was becoming alarmed.

'I told you that I wasn't to be disturbed under any circumstances,' he growled.

Placidly she agreed. 'Yes, sir.'

'Then kindly adhere to my orders.'

She placed two plump hands on her

ample hips. In a motherly voice and with the familiarity of one who had given long and faithful service she pointed out that a man could not be expected to work on an empty stomach.

'You have had nothing to eat since breakfast, sir.'

'And you have interrupted my train of thought just when I am in the middle of a particularly complicated murder investigation.'

Unrepentant, Mrs Nibela made a suitable apology. 'Dinner,' she told him disapprovingly, 'will be held back until ten o'clock tonight, according to your instructions.' Really, whatever would the boy want next?

That the *boy* was thirty-three years old mattered not to Mrs Nibela; she still watched over him like a mother hen, having worked for his parents since before he was born. When the professor had inherited Dargle Park, the large red brick homestead with its surrounding fields, she'd stayed on as his housekeeper. She considered herself to be part of the furniture and there wasn't a family secret to which she wasn't party.

The professor nodded absently, his eyes glued to the computer screen.

'Agnes will leave a chicken casserole for you in the oven and there's a nice little treacle tart with custard for afterwards,' she added hopefully.

'Whatever.' His tones held faint irritation. His housekeeper meant well but she appeared to have a thing about feeding him! He could do without having to think about food right now when the murder weapon had just been discovered in a hospital laundry basket, covered in blood . . .

A few minutes later he rose from the desk in utter frustration and stood staring out into the garden with unseeing eyes; it was a beautiful garden, brilliant with summer bougainvillea.

'Darned woman! Where the dickens was I?' he muttered, trying to recapture the flow of words. 'Oh, right. The knife . . . '

He took a deep breath and forced himself to concentrate.

Um . . . *The laundry worker gazed uncomprehendingly at the knife. It lay, thick with congealed blood, against the stark whiteness of the sheet; a vicious agent of destruction.* He paused. 'No, dash it, that doesn't sound right . . . '

Unfazed by her abrupt dismissal, Mrs Nibela made her way down the long passage to the kitchen to ensure that Agnes, the new cook, hadn't forgotten to put the mushrooms in the casserole. The professor was particularly fond of mushrooms.

As she opened the door her mouth tightened. Agnes, in her opinion, was far too nosey. She must not be allowed to discover any of Professor Gray's secrets.

'Nothing but work, work, work,' she muttered to herself in exasperation. 'What normal man eats his dinner at ten o'clock? He needs a wife to turn him into a human being again.'

Agnes was standing at the Aga,

stirring the soup. Her ears were sharper than her wits.

'Professor Gray already has a wife,' she pointed out in their own language.

Mrs Nibela's head snapped up. 'What did you say?'

Something in the housekeeper's face told Agnes she had spoken out of turn. Hurriedly she turned her attention to the pan.

'N-nothing.'

'Agnes, kindly repeat what you have just said,' Mrs Nibela demanded.

Agnes hesitated. 'I said the boss already has a wife.' She added a little defiantly. 'Well, he must have a wife.'

'Why?'

'He has a child, hasn't he? He must have a wife if he has a child.'

'So?'

Agnes began to look uncomfortable. 'Well . . . everybody says he has a wife, it's just that she doesn't live with him and that's the reason we don't see her around. Everybody says it's that blonde woman who comes here and asks him for money. She gets the money and then goes straight back to Johannesburg and buys all those fabulous clothes.'

Mrs Nibela's tones were icy. 'Indeed.'

'The blonde woman says the professor is very mean; he doesn't give her enough money. At least, that's what she told the hairdresser in the village, and the hairdresser told my aunt, who works there. Everybody says he must be a very stingy man ... ' she trailed off uncertainly.

Mrs Nibela's mouth was a tight, angry line, completely at odds with her normal cheery smile.

'By 'everybody' you mean the people who live in Howick,' she snapped. 'Those people ought to mind their own business. They know nothing about anything! You have been listening to too much gossip, my good girl, and if you wish to keep your job at Dargle Park I advise you to concentrate on your cooking and leave the subject of wives well alone, is that clear? Professor Gray has enough troubles as it is.'

'Yes, Mrs Nibela,' Agnes agreed meekly. She hurried into the scullery and rolled her eyes heavenwards.

Mrs Nibela followed her with a stern warning. 'You are not to repeat any of this to young Master Jamie, is that clear?'

'Who is Master Jamie?'

Mrs Nibela hesitated. 'The professor's . . . son. You will meet him when he returns from school tomorrow afternoon.'

Unaware of his housekeeper's culinary musings, Jonathan Gray continued to stare into the garden, feeling as frustrated as a woodpecker in a petrified forest.

'Heaven preserve me from housekeepers,' he growled, returning to the desk to close the file he'd been working on. 'Why can't they leave a man in peace?'

His concentration had been well and truly broken. Whenever the flow of words dried up he knew what he must do: ride out to the foothills of the Drakensberg Mountains and take a long walk before the light faded. The crisp mountain air and the majestic beauty of the landscape would restore his creative energies.

He shrugged his powerful shoulders into a brown leather jacket and reached for the keys of his Harley Davidson motor cycle. Hopefully when he returned the fresh air would have blown away all his mental cobwebs and he would be able to complete chapter four before Jamie came home tomorrow.

'Face it, Gray,' he mocked as he fastened the strap of his black protective helmet, 'if that so-called fancy brain of yours can come up with a solution to this hideous crime, you'll be smarter than a tree full of owls.'

A spasm crossed his handsome face. At least his work had distracted him from the unpleasant decision he must soon make; this evening, if possible . . .

★　★　★

Marissa Boyd walked to the edge of the large, tangled garden and gazed into the distance. She had forgotten how sharply the ancient, jagged peaks of the mighty Drakensberg Mountains pierced the sky. According to legend they were the abode of dragons, hence the name, Dragon Mountains. They formed one of the most spectacular attractions in all of South Africa.

As the distant backdrop to her new home they were etched now in sepia against the fading sky. As she watched, the last fiery rays of the sun drained away and the instant chill of dusk settled on her shoulders, forcing her back up the slate path to the tiny cottage.

Mellow red brick under thatch, with cascading yellow roses about the front door, it was a charming reminder of another age. On his retirement her grandfather had purchased the cottage from Dargle Park, the large country estate which adjoined it. It was her grandmother who had planted the roses around the door and after her death Grandfather had kept them looking glorious year after year with his meticulous feeding and pruning . . . until now, when sadly, they were looking rather the worse for wear.

Marissa blinked away the sudden moisture in her eyes.

'Please get better soon, Grandfather,' she murmured, 'Rose Cottage is not the same without you.'

Feisty and independent, he hadn't said a word about his state of health until it had been too late, and now he was in the hospital in Pietermaritzburg. When he came out he would need careful nursing, which was why she was here.

It was obvious to her that he'd been unwell for months and hadn't been able to see to things properly. Both the garden and the cottage had become run down, and the electricity had recently been switched off.

'At least the property is still in Boyd hands,' Marissa told herself briskly.

It would remain so, too, if she had anything to do with it! According to her grandfather their unpleasant neighbour had paid him a visit and tried to coerce him into selling it back to the estate. He'd been rather upset about it at the time and the stress had doubtless contributed to his heart problems.

It was dark inside the house. Marissa told herself robustly that it didn't faze her in the least. The cottage may be isolated but no-one knew she was there, did they? Besides, there were blankets on the beds and she would be warm enough with her cat, Mrs Tipper, sleeping at her feet. In the morning she would drive to the nearby village of Howick to arrange for the electricity to be reconnected and until then she'd use a stub of candle she'd spied earlier in one of the kitchen drawers.

Cleaning materials would have to be purchased too because her grandfather's stock of commodities was pitifully small. Unable to abide disorder, Marissa determined that she would make a start of the grubby interior as soon as possible.

She sighed. If only she'd known how things stood she'd have given up her job long before now and come to live with her grandfather. She was, after all, his only living relative, and to be honest, she'd been toying with the idea of a move for months. It was her grandfather's illness coupled with Tippy's condition which had finally made her take the plunge.

Tippy, it appeared, had taken up with Tiger, the one-eyed tomcat from next door. The result of this unfortunate liaison was the imminent arrival of a litter of kittens. How could Tippy, who showed all signs of being an excellent mother, be expected to raise her small family on the balcony of a high-rise apartment block in the middle of Durban?

So Marissa had given a term's notice at the school where she'd been teaching, packed up her belongings and undertaken the two-hour car journey inland from the coast to the wilds of rural Kwa Zulu Natal. Not only would she be on hand to look after her grandfather when he came out of hospital, but it would also give her the opportunity to follow a long-held dream.

'I can't wait to set up my business,' she informed Tippy as she searched for a box of matches in order to light the candle.

'Of course, the car will have to live under the acacia tree at the back but Grandfather won't mind,' Marissa explained. 'It's just that I must have the double garage as my studio.'

She'd brought with her the pottery wheel, electric kiln and precious collection of glazed pots she'd been at pains to stockpile over the past year, and as soon as she had enough wares to sell she intended to open her little factory-cum-shop.

'I'll place a sign at the front gate saying *Rose Cottage Pottery*. It's a good enough name, don't you think,

Tippy? As soon as we're settled in I shall go into Howick and find a sign writer.'

She would have no trouble in attracting customers. It was fortunate that the cottage was situated on the *Midlands Meander*; a long, winding route through the countryside; popular with city-dwellers as an area famous for its unique mix of over a hundred craft shops and quaint eating places.

'There won't be a shortage of tourists all looking for interesting things to buy before Christmas,' she added happily. 'I'll have to get busy, won't I?'

Outside, the light had faded swiftly, as it always did in Africa. Marissa closed the kitchen curtains and lit the candle, setting it in a saucer on the worktop so she could see while she scrabbled in the box of supplies for a tin of cat food.

After her own meal she intended to take a cold shower and then dive straight into bed even though it was still a little early. She would dearly love to have continued reading her novel but her curiosity would have to be contained until tomorrow. There was little point in reading by such meagre light even though she was simply dying to find out what happened next to the hero, a private investigator by the name of Brett Morgan of the Ace Detective Agency. He'd just rushed into a strange house and apprehended a beautiful woman in her own home in the mistaken belief that she was an intruder. The woman would turn out to be the heroine, of course, and they would fall madly in love . . .

Marissa sighed. Brett Morgan was such a hunk! It was just as well he wasn't flesh and blood or she'd be in big trouble.

'Such a marvellous man,' she murmured ten minutes later as she emerged from the bathroom. 'If he were real, Tippy, he'd have the women queuing up till kingdom come, I can tell you. And I'd be the first in the queue.'

She finished wiping the surfaces and

was about to return to the bedroom when she heard a faint sound. It came from just outside the kitchen door; a slow, stealthy tread on the pebbles. Marissa's blood turned to ice.

'Oh, s-stinging s-scorpions,' she gulped, her breath catching in her throat. She always stuttered when she was scared.

Who could be prowling around in Grandfather's garden at this time of night? The cottage was isolated, too. Her nearest neighbour lived some way up the hill in a huge red brick mansion out of sight behind a stand of pine trees. And judging from the way he'd treated her grandfather he was a nasty individual.

The soft, scraping sound ceased abruptly. It was almost as though the owner of the footsteps was listening, too. Marissa felt her legs tremble, and gripped the counter for support. It was then that she remembered her cell phone battery had run down earlier. She couldn't summon help even if she tried.

Desperately she tried to gather her courage. If only Brett Morgan were here just at this moment!

'Oh, help. Think clearly, Marissa,' she ordered herself. Some instinct told her to pinch out the candlelight. It left her standing in the darkness as she cautiously lifted one corner of the curtain to peer outside. But at that precise moment the moon rode behind a bank of clouds and she couldn't see a thing.

Her mouth was dry with fright. The door was locked but nevertheless she needed some sort of weapon, just in case . . . like that broomstick leaning against one wall in the corner. It wasn't much, but it was better than nothing. Soundlessly Marissa whipped it from its place. At all costs Tippy had to be protected.

Poised at the ready, her heart jerked painfully as a different type of scraping noise sounded in her ears. It was a key turning stealthily in the lock. Horrified, she watched as the door handle slowly began to turn and the shocking truth penetrated her terrified mind that somebody else had a key to Rose Cottage.

The door was inched open until it was wide enough for her to distinguish the giant of a man standing on the doorstep. The moon emerged from behind the clouds and showed him slinking into the room with all the grace of a leopard stalking its prey.

With a spine-chilling shriek she sprang at the intruder and delivered a hard, satisfying thwack on the skull.

The man gave a shout of pain and leapt backwards, holding his head.

Much encouraged, Marissa lifted the broomstick to hit him again. This time he warded off the blow as though it was nothing more than an annoying insect. In a lightning quick movement he yanked her arms behind her back and pinned her roughly against the wall.

'What the blazes do you think you're doing, young man?' His voice was deep and furious. 'I'd like to knock your filthy teeth down your throat! If you weren't such a puny young man I'd teach you a lesson you aren't likely to forget.'

'What did you expect?' Marissa spat, her voice shrill with fright. 'I'd like to knock your teeth down your throat, too!'

The man's arms dropped quickly to his sides. He stared in disbelief.

'Great heaven, you're a woman!'

Marissa glared back, her chest heaving with fright.

'So?' she challenged.

He wasted no time in thrusting one hand into a pocket and withdrawing a small torch. When he'd flashed the light into her face and raked it with his narrowed gaze, he drawled, 'I amend that to yelling, demented shrew.'

'Take that light out of my eyes at once,' Marissa snapped. She'd never felt so terrified in her life. Now that he realised she was a woman, and all alone in the cottage, what would he do?

The light moved, sweeping her from

head to foot. A compelling blue gaze flicked her over in an ostensibly impersonal manner but it was enough to make Marissa feel he had taken in every detail of her appearance.

His gaze fastened once more on her face. It widened as he registered the glossy dark hair, fine bone structure and soft, pink lips. The mutiny blazing in her large green eyes was every bit as fascinating as the angry colour flagging her cheekbones.

Unexpectedly, the breath locked in Jonathan Gray's chest. He shook his head in disbelief. People said he had a mind like a steel trap but at this moment it had obviously ceased to function. All he could think of was that fascinating little dimple in that firm little chin . . .

'How do you do?' he muttered, feeling the greatest fool this side of the Limpopo River.

Marissa gazed back fearfully before screwing up her eyes. 'I said take that torchlight off my face.'

To her surprise he quickly complied, placing the torch on the corner so that its beam cast concentric circles on the dingy kitchen ceiling. Quite unable to resist a quick, reciprocal scrutiny of this frightening stranger, Marissa tried to think where she'd seen him before. Despite looking like a pirate in need of a shave he was a distinctly impressive male.

The penny dropped. She gave a quick gasp. Of course! He looked just like Pierce Brosnan, the movie star, only his chin was tougher and his hair longer.

'Who . . . who are you?' she quavered, annoyed to find that her voice was still shrill with nerves.

He didn't answer. Instead, he took his time in viewing her with considerable interest from a great height.

Marissa gasped. 'Get out of my house,' she said furiously, 'or I'll . . . I'll . . . '

'Your house?' He laughed nastily. 'This cottage belongs to a friend of mine who happens to be away from home at the moment. I was passing when I saw a faint light inside and decided to investigate.' His lips thinned into a tight line. 'And what do I find? A beautiful little criminal intent on brazening it out in the hopes that I'll go away.'

He grabbed her firmly by the elbow. 'You're leaving this property at once, and I shall personally escort you off it. I suggest you find a more constructive use for your time than breaking and entering.' His lip curled scornfully. 'Why not get yourself a decent job? You might even learn to become a useful member of society.'

'Of all the nerve,' Marissa hissed.

'Can you not see you're made for better things than this?'

At that moment Tippy appeared from the bedroom. She paused, looked him over disdainfully and sashayed over to her bowl of milk for a nightcap.

Marissa seized the opportunity to twist out of his grasp. 'See? Even Mrs Tippet thinks you're a nutter,' she taunted, 'and she's a good judge of character.' Except in the case of Tiger, perhaps, but he didn't need to know about that.

The man's eyes widened. 'You bring your cat with you on these unsavoury jaunts? Lady, you're the fruitcake!'

'No kidding,' Marissa jeered. 'At least I don't go round accosting innocent women in their homes. If you don't leave immediately I'll . . . I'll . . . '

He folded his brown leather-clad arms across his chest and gazed at her as though she were an interesting bug he'd found in his tea.

'You'll what?'

Rattled, Marissa said the first thing which came into her head. 'I'll . . . I'll telephone my friend, Brett Morgan.'

His mouth dropped open. 'Who . . . ?'

'Brett Morgan. He's a private investigator and he'll sort you out plenty pronto.'

He blinked. 'Did you . . . say Brett Morgan?'

'Yes, I said Brett Morgan. You'd

better go at once, because when Brett Morgan gets here you will end up feeling extremely sorry for yourself.'

Marissa was mortified to find that her voice had begun to wobble. She'd had a very stressful day what with having to pack up her Durban flat and drive ninety miles inland only to find a filthy house at the other end, with no utilities. And on top of that her beloved grandfather was ill. And now this creep was accosting her at the dead of night and he had a key to the cottage and tomorrow she'd be forced to have all the locks changed . . . it was all becoming too much!

The man was looking at her strangely. 'Tell me about this friend, Brett Morgan,' he coaxed.

Marissa took a deep, steadying breath. If she could keep talking she'd try to get him near enough to the door to push him out and then quickly lock it by shoving her own key in the lock . . . that way, he wouldn't be able to come back inside. Her own key was hanging where she'd left it, on its hook next to the door.

'Well, like I said, he's a private investigator. He bumps off any undesirables who get in his way so you'd better watch it, mister. He . . . he lives down the road, actually,' she improvised desperately.

A spasm crossed his face. 'He does?'

'Oh, yes. In fact, he's due to visit me at any moment, and if he finds you here he'll be very, very angry. He's the jealous type, you see.'

Marissa gabbled on, quite forgetting where she was; living her role as heroine to the full. Her eyes glowed with green fire and her voice grew husky with excitement.

Jonathan Gray, unable to take his eyes off her, found himself utterly intrigued.

His eyebrows rose when Marissa announced blithely, 'We're engaged to be married, you know.'

By this time Tippy had finished her milk. She decided that the visitor was acceptable after all, and proceeded to rub herself against one of his long, jeans-encased legs. Absently Jonathan picked her up and held her against his chest.

'This . . . Brett Morgan,' he asked in a strange voice, 'does he know of your criminal activities?'

Marissa's smile disappeared. The fascinating emerald fire became a hostile green flare. 'How many times must I say it? I am no intruder. I live here.'

His mouth tightened in sudden disdain. 'Garbage!'

Marissa, normally sweet-tempered, found it difficult to control the fury which finally erupted after her very stressful day.

'It's not garbage,' she yelled. 'Rose Cottage belongs to my grandfather, Henry Boyd, who happens to be in St Anne's hospital at this moment — you can phone up and verify the facts for yourself. I have only just arrived and I'm here to stay, complete with cat, whether you like it or not.'

Her eyes blinked furiously. 'I have no idea who you are but if you're an example of the kind of person who lives around here then I'll be keeping myself very much to myself in future. I can do without people like you in my life!'

Slowly Johnathan bent down and placed Tippy on the floor. When he straightened, a dull tide of red had crept above the collar of his blue polo shirt.

He said in an appalled voice, 'Henry Boyd is really your grandfather?' He swallowed hard. 'Would you mind telling me your name?'

'Marissa Jane Boyd.'

He took a deep breath and expelled it slowly. 'Yes. I thought it must be.'

'Is that a problem?'

'On the contrary. Henry is very proud of you.'

What Henry hadn't said was that his granddaughter lived in a world of dreams. The old man might be past his sell-by date but he was still sharp as a scythe, and down to earth with it. Who would have thought his charming granddaughter had a couple of vacant rooms in the upper story?

Wariness warred with bewilderment in Marissa's eyes. 'You know my grandfather?'

'He's a close friend of mine and he has often spoken of you. It seems I owe you an enormous apology, Miss Boyd. Please understand that I was acting in your grandfather's best interests. I thought you were an intruder. I am sorry to have bothered you.'

He appeared to be so genuinely regretful that Marissa, a kind girl at heart, found her anger being replaced by a tremendous sense of relief. However, she wasn't about to let him off lightly.

'I will excuse your extraordinary behaviour,' she said coldly, 'as long as you leave my house immediately.'

He unclipped a key from his key ring and handed it over. 'Allow me to return this. Your grandfather wanted me to have it in case of any emergencies, but I have no use for it now that you're here. Have you any idea when he'll be coming home?'

'No.'

Despite her antipathy towards him she was suddenly reluctant to see the back of this strange, compelling man. Who on earth was he?

As though he'd read her mind he thrust out a hand and said quickly, 'My name is Gray. Jonathan Gray.'

'Good night, Mr Gray,' she said firmly, and closed the door.

Hearing her key turn hastily in the lock, Jonathan laughed softly. It was a long time since he'd been issued with such firm marching orders by such a desirable female. His shoulders were still shaking when he reached the motorcycle he'd left parked out of sight on the grass verge. He revved the engine and drove the short distance up the road to his home, the large, red brick house tucked away behind a stand of pine trees.

There would be no need, he reflected, to inform Miss Boyd that he was not only Jonathan Gray but also DJ Grayson, best-selling author. Or more to the point, creator of the Brett Morgan series.

He couldn't think of anything more delightful than having the captivating Miss Boyd on his doorstep. For one thing, she was in love with Brett Morgan!

'Brett, old boy.' He grinned as the Harley nosed through the gateposts of his home. 'If I were a free man you'd be getting ready to encounter some hefty opposition right now. The lady represents a challenge few men could resist.'

By the time he'd negotiated the drive up to the house and parked his motorcycle in one of the garages between the silver Mercedes and the dark green Range Rover, the grin had disappeared.

Much as it galled him to admit it, he did not consider himself to be a free man.

He had Jamie to think of.

# 2

Jonathan let himself into the house and went into the kitchen to find the promised casserole which Agnes had left for him in the Aga. He served up a large portion and took his plate into the formal dining-room where he was accustomed to dining alone.

For once his thoughts were not centred upon his work. Much to his chagrin they were firmly fixed on Marissa Boyd. He simply couldn't get her out of his mind. She was one of the most exquisite young women he had ever laid eyes on and those appealing green eyes left him feeling breathless.

Much as he hated to admit it, she lit a spark in him. For a start her imagination was delightful. He was a man who couldn't abide stolid, unimaginative types, and the very fact that Marissa Boyd was able to enter so wholeheartedly into his fantasy world meant that she was a female after his own heart. How ironic it was that he should at last find a woman who captivated him just when he had decided to marry Jamie's mother!

His jaw clenched in frustration.

It was an abominable situation. Marriage or nothing, Nerina had told him in no uncertain terms. For months she'd cajoled, sulked and then finally threatened: either marry her by Christmas, she'd told him, or she would disappear for good and take Jamie with her, in which case he would never see the child again; a scenario which didn't bear thinking about.

Nerina Gray, the widow of his late brother, Charles, had been after him ever since she'd discovered the size of his bank balance. He was under no illusions about her, either. She was a fickle, scheming woman who had married Charles for his money. What's more, she was the type of woman who craved fame as well as fortune. If she received any inkling of his true identity she'd have no hesitation in exposing him to the world. This was one of the reasons he guarded his secret so fiercely. Apart from his immediate family, only his publisher and solicitor knew who he really was.

'Confounded woman,' he muttered grimly as he poured himself a cup of coffee. He had no wish to be shackled for life to a woman like Nerina, but as he saw it he had no option. She was calling all the shots, knowing full well he'd promised his dying brother that he would act as a father to Jamie. She knew him well enough, too, to know he'd keep that promise if it killed him.

Jamie had suffered unbelievably when his father had died and knowing that his mother had little time for him, had turned to his uncle for comfort. Jonathan had consequently vowed that even if it meant the sacrifice of his personal freedom he could and would not fail the child now.

Jonathan took his cup of coffee into

the study; not that he'd be able to write a word in his present frame of mind.

Now that he'd met Marissa Boyd it was more than ever imperative that he stop dithering and marry Nerina at the earliest opportunity. He couldn't afford to allow himself the luxury of getting to know his new neighbour given the fact that she attracted him like a kid to a candy store. He was an honourable man, and it would be asking for trouble.

He and Nerina would tie the knot quietly some time in the next few weeks and then take Jamie to Switzerland for Christmas where some winter sports would restore his spirits. He'd teach Jamie to ski while his new wife kept out of his way, making inroads into his bank account with one of her unbridled shopping sprees. At least he wouldn't be expected to entertain the woman.

Jonathan flopped into an armchair and closed his eyes.

Nerina, he reflected cynically, wouldn't be unduly bothered when he informed her it was to be a marriage in name only. She would doubtless return to her work in Johannesburg at the earliest convenience where she had a flock of mindless friends to entertain her.

Once his new 'wife' had departed he would return to his writing and keep his mind firmly on his work. He wouldn't give Miss Boyd another thought. In fact, he'd go out of his way to ensure that he never set eyes on her again.

★　★　★

Jamie Grayson stood on the front steps of the school, suitcase in hand, waiting for his Uncle Jonathan to fetch him. One large tear crept down his cheek. Afraid to be seen crying in front of the other boys, he dashed it away fiercely.

The truth was he hated school. He hated the rowdy bullies in the dormitory, he hated the grim-faced matron who smelt of mothballs and he hated the awful porridge they made him eat every morning. On top of it all, he was missing his dad.

He brightened as he recognised the green Land Rover which came purring up the school drive. Uncle Jonathan had come to take him home! Uncle Jonathan would tell him he needn't go back to school ever again . . .

'Hello, old man,' Jonathan greeted his nephew warmly. He clapped Jamie on the shoulder and pretended not to see the tear-stained cheeks. 'Everything OK?'

'N-not really,' Jamie muttered.

'You can tell me all about it later,' Jonathan said gently. 'In the meantime, how about a trip to McDonald's on the way home?'

He leaned over to buckle Jamie's seatbelt and suggested casually, 'After lunch we could take in a movie if you like.'

Suddenly the day seemed brighter. Jamie glanced up at his uncle adoringly. Uncle Jonathan knew just how to make him feel better!

'I'm glad you're my new dad,' Jamie

told his uncle sharply when they were in the car. 'I feel safe when you're around. You won't go away, will you?'

Jonathan swallowed the sudden lump in his throat and kept his eyes on the road ahead. 'No, I won't go away,' he promised lightly.

He continued evenly, 'It's perfectly all right to miss your dad, you know, Jamie. I miss him too, but we'll make out just fine, you'll see.'

As the Land Rover headed for Howick Jamie looked thoughtful. 'When is my mother coming to see me again?'

Jonathan hesitated. 'Well, she's very busy just now, but I'm sure she'll be along as soon as she can. In the meantime we'll have some fun this weekend, you and I.'

Jamie shook his head. 'I don't think that will be possible.' Once again he looked near to tears.

'Oh? Why not?'

'I have a whole six exercises of mathematics to do, and I hate mathematics!'

Jonathan shot him a narrowed glance. 'This is your holiday, Jamie. Why the homework?'

Jamie gulped. 'Old Bucky doesn't like me, that's why.'

'Old Bucky?'

'Mr Buckworth. He's our maths master. I'm the only one who has to do maths homework and it's because he doesn't like me.' His large blue eyes filled with tears.

'Was it not because you were slow in finishing the work during class today?'

'Well, I suppose. Trouble is, I was slow because I don't understand how to do it, and the other boys were laughing at me. I hate them when they laugh at me, and I hate Old Bucky. He's a mean, mean man.'

He gave a great sniff. 'I hate boarding school, Uncle Jonathan.' His eyes were imploring. 'Please may I live with you at Dargle Park? I could go to the day school in Howick. You could drive me there everyday and I promise to be very, very, good.'

Jonathan's heart constricted in compassion. The child had lost a good deal of confidence and was in great need of reassurance. At the age of eight it couldn't be easy coping with a father's death and the disdain of a selfish, absentee mother.

'I'll talk it over with your mother,' Jonathan promised, 'but right now Jamie, we are going to enjoy ourselves. Let's forget all about school and concentrate on food, shall we? I'm starving and I'm sure you must be, too.'

★   ★   ★

It was a glorious spring day with the late October sunshine gilding the distant mountains and the sound of cooing doves in the acacia trees behind the cottage.

Immensely satisfied with her morning's work, Marissa paused to wipe her perspiring forehead before taking a long drink of water. She'd cleaned Rose Cottage from front to back and it was as pristine as she could make it. The dust had even been wiped from the heavy oak under the thatch in the living-room.

'After lunch, Tippy, I shall sweep out the garage and when that's done there's the front lawn to be tackled.'

Like her late grandfather, she didn't believe in allowing the grass to grow under her feet — literally! He'd left an almost new mower in the garden shed, for which she was heartily grateful. The lawn had grown at an alarming rate as a result of the spring rains.

'Come along, Tippy,' she sang gaily as she took her tray of ham sandwiches out to the wrought iron garden furniture which stood on the tiny patio beside the living-room.

She put down the tray and proudly poured a cup of tea from the blue ceramic teapot she'd moulded and glazed only a few weeks ago.

Marissa was stirring her tea when a movement caught her eye. Startled, she looked up to see a small boy gazing at her, his head just visible above the gate. His shock of dark hair stood on end rather endearingly and his blue eyes were bright with curiosity.

'Who are you talking to?' he asked.

Marissa put down her teaspoon. 'Hello. I'm talking to my cat.'

'Why? Cat's can't answer back.'

'No, but I'm sure she understands me, and it's nice to have someone to talk to. I'm not lonely when I can talk to my cat.'

'I'm always lonely,' he informed her unselfconsciously.

'Are you? Perhaps you need a cat or dog. Pets are good company, you know. You're never lonely if you have a pet.'

'What's your cat's name?'

'Mrs Tippet. I call her Tippy, for short.'

'May I come in and stroke her?'

Marissa smiled. 'Of course you may, if she'll let you.'

The boy opened the gate and ran up to the table where upon Tippy, quite put out by the unexpected visitor, made like a missile into the house.

'She doesn't like me,' he observed gravely.

'It's not that, it's just that she's a little frightened of strangers.'

He was examining the sandwiches with an interested eye. 'Are you having your lunch?'

'Yes. Would you like a sandwich? They're ham and tomato.'

'Yes, please.' He accepted a sandwich, took a large bite and introduced himself through a mouthful of ham. 'My name's Jamie.'

Marissa, who loved children, hadn't realised how much she had been missing them since giving up her teaching job.

'Mine's Marissa Boyd. Do you live around here, Jamie?'

He nodded before wolfing down the rest of the sandwich as though it were his last meal on earth.

'I haven't been hungry at all up until now,' he explained. 'May I have another one, please?'

'Of course.' Marissa passed him the plate, wondering who his parents were and why they allowed him to roam the countryside so freely. Small boys exploring isolated country roads were not exactly an everyday occurrence in these parts.

'Where do you live, Jamie?'

'At Dargle Park. At least, I live there when I'm not away at school. It's the big red brick house up the road.' He pointed in the direction of the distant stand of pines. 'You can just see the chimney pots above the trees. I live there with my uncle. My dad,' he volunteered sadly, 'is dead.'

Marissa's heart sank. 'I'm sorry to hear it. Mine's dead, too, and my mother, so I know how it feels.'

'My mother's almost dead,' he told her matter-of-factly. 'She lives in Johannesburg, and that's as good as being dead, isn't it?'

Startled, Marissa murmured something vague.

Jamie looked her over with interest.

'Do you live with your uncle, too?'

'No, I live alone . . . for the moment.'

'Here?'

'Yes, here at Rose Cottage.'

'My uncle told me an old man lived at Rose Cottage.'

'That's correct. My grandfather has lived here for many years, but he's ill in hospital at the moment. I'm hoping he'll be back again soon. Would you like a cup of tea? I can fetch another cup.'

Jamie shook his head. 'No, thank you, I wouldn't want to trouble you.'

Marvelling at the child's good manners, Marissa gave him a warm smile. 'Oh, it's no trouble.'

'All the same, no thanks.'

When she asked about his school a moment later, Jamie's expression darkened.

'I don't like my school,' he said, misery evident in his eyes, 'I've got maths homework this week and I don't understand how to do it. I know I'll get it all wrong and then I'll get detention from Old Bucky when I go back.' He gave a heavy sigh. 'I just hate fractions.'

This was too good an opportunity to miss. Marissa loved teaching and besides, she was rather taken with this charming child.

'I know a way to make fractions really fun.' She smiled. 'I used to be a teacher, you know, and I have all sorts of interesting things in my special apparatus box. Old Bucky,' she added craftily, 'will turn blue when you hand in your homework and he sees that all the answers are correct.'

Jamie beamed. 'Cool! You'll really help me?'

'Sure.'

'That's great! I'll go home for lunch and then I'll come back with my books, if that's all right with you?'

Marissa thought of all the tasks she had intended to do and mentally shelved them. The child's smile was reward enough in itself.

'I'll be waiting for you, Jamie,' she promised.

Jamie swallowed the last of his

sandwich. 'Thanks again, Miss Boyd,' he told her fervently.

'No problem. And Jamie . . . '

'Yes?'

'I wouldn't like to have to answer to your uncle for feeding you those ham sandwiches just before lunch. Be sure to eat all your food.'

He grinned. 'Leave that to me, Miss Boyd.'

It was amazing, Jamie thought as he scooted up the road towards Dargle Park, he hadn't been at all hungry until he'd met Miss Boyd, and now he could eat an elephant!

Jonathan was on the telephone in the study when he entered the house and ran upstairs to wash his hands, to reappear in the dining-room just as Mrs Nibela was carefully placing a dish of salad on the large mahogany table.

'Is that all?' he asked, disappointment evident on his flushed face.

The housekeeper hid a smile. 'I thought you said you weren't hungry today, Jamie.'

47

'Oh, that was this morning. I'm very hungry now, Nibby.'

'I'm very glad to hear it.'

Hiding her satisfaction, she went to the kitchen and returned with a platter of assorted cold meats. 'There's jelly afterwards and I've made some flapjacks for afternoon tea.'

Jamie flung his arms around her waist. 'I love flapjacks!'

'Yes, I know, that's why I made them.' She laughed.

Suddenly he remembered Miss Boyd and the mathematics.

'I may be a little late for tea, Nibby. I have a date after lunch with a very pretty lady.'

Mrs Nibela chuckled. 'Then I will keep some flapjacks, but make sure you are not too late.'

Her glance was indulgent as she added, 'Which pretty lady? The one on television who tells you all those wildlife stories?'

Jamie grinned. 'She's not on the telly, Nibby, she's in real life and she's the most beautiful lady I've ever seen. Her eyes are green and her hair is black and she has a cat called Tippy. My uncle Jonathan should marry her.'

'Go on with you,' Mrs Nibela laughed, not believing a word.

She went back to the kitchen for the sliced bread and informed a mystified Agnes, 'That boy Jamie is just like the professor. He lives in another world.'

Jonathan replaced the receiver just as the gong went for lunch. He took a deep, angry breath and raked a hand through his dark hair. He could strangle Nerina! She'd just informed him that she hadn't the slightest interest in discussing Jamie's schooling problems. She was too busy establishing herself as a fashion photographer and as far as she was concerned he was paying good money to a private school for her son's education. What more could the child expect? If Jamie hadn't settled into his new school then it was up to Jonathan to ensure that he did. One way or the other, she was not to be bothered.

'Fine,' Jonathan had grated, unable to keep the disgust from his voice, 'I will deal with the situation as I think fit. Another thing, Nerina,' he'd told her firmly, 'it's time you took a few days off work and visited your son. He needs a mother's support right now.'

'I'm not very maternal, Jonathan, and well you know it. I can hear that you're just a teensy weensy bit grumpy today. It'll be all that typing or whatever it is you do in your study. Very well, I'll see what I can do, but if I visit Dargle Park it certainly won't be Jamie that I'm keen to see . . . ' she allowed her voice to trail off huskily.

Jonathan schooled his features into a bland mask and took himself into the dining-room where he chatted amiably with Jamie throughout the meal. To his relief the child appeared to be much happier, tucking into the food with surprising gusto.

Jamie gabbled on about cats and dogs and then informed his uncle that he'd like a cat because you couldn't possibly be lonely if you had a cat to talk to.

'Oh, quite,' Jonathan agreed gravely.

When there was no more chicken to be eaten, Jonathan offered Jamie a bowl of red jelly.

'Aren't you having any desert, Uncle Jonathan?'

'No, thank you, Jamie. I'm not partial to jelly.'

'Then may I have yours as well? I'm really hungry today.'

Hiding his surprise, Jonathan readily agreed. Whatever had wrought this pleasing change? Yesterday at McDonalds, Jamie had picked at his food.

He served up another large helping of jelly and drenched it with custard. 'I'm glad to see you enjoying your lunch.'

'Well, Nibby says a man can't work on an empty stomach,' Jamie told him seriously, 'and I have a lot of work to do this afternoon.'

'You do?'

'I'll be so busy that I may be late for tea, Uncle Jonathan, but don't you worry, I've already told Nibby all about it and she'll be keeping my flapjacks until I'm ready for them.'

Jonathan hid his relief. 'In that case, you don't mind if I disappear into the study? I had intended for us to spend some time together this afternoon but as you'll be otherwise occupied, I might as well do a spot of work.'

'Not at all, Uncle Jonathan,' Jamie agreed graciously. 'I'll see you later.' He folded his table napkin and politely asked to be excused from the table.

* * *

It was four hours later that Mrs Nibela tapped on the study door.

Jonathan looked up absently. 'Yes?'

'I'm a little concerned about Master Jamie,' she said. 'He's not been around all afternoon and he didn't come in for his tea.'

Jonathan raked a hand through his hair and tried not to feel irritated. His housekeeper was fussing again!

'Have you looked in his bedroom? He told me he had a lot of work to do and I presumed it was homework.'

'Agnes and I have looked everywhere, sir. He is not in his bedroom.'

Jonathan frowned. 'I'll have a quick look around the garden.' He closed his file and stood up. 'Don't worry, Mrs Nibela, he'll be around somewhere. He knows he's not to go outside these grounds.'

Confident that he knew exactly where Jamie was, he strode out of the front door and around the side of the building to the big oak tree where he and Charles had constructed a tree house for Jamie last summer.

'Jamie,' he called.

When there was no reply Jonathan scanned the garden and set off at a brisk trot, calling out as he went. When he'd scouted the entire grounds without success he went to find the Zulu gardener, Alpheus.

The old man looked up from his weeding and greeted Jonathan politely.

'Master Jamie? Yes, I saw him earlier, sir. He went down the road.'

'When was this?'

'Straight after lunch, sir.'

Jonathan went pale. Surely the child had not taken it into his head to run away? If that were the case then by this time he'd be half way to Howick, always supposing some stranger hadn't already picked him up.

He raced into the house for the keys of his motor cycle, pulling on his helmet as he hurried through the hall. A moment later he accelerated down the drive, intent on scouring all the roads in the vicinity as soon as possible.

Before he'd gone ten yards from the gate he was forced to a sudden, screeching halt.

Jamie, still beaming, stood gazing up at him, his school books in one hand and a pile of chocolate chip cookies in the other.

Jonathan controlled the angry retort which sprang to his lips, took a deep breath and enquired smoothly, 'Where have you been, young man?'

Jamie's smile became broader. 'She gave me chocolate chip cookies, Uncle Jonathan, and she said I can go there any time, and I know how to do fractions now, they're easy-peasy. Old Bucky's going to turn blue . . . ?'

'Who?' Jonathan demanded. 'Who gave you cookies? Where have you been?'

'I've been to see Miss Boyd at Rose Cottage. She said — '

'Never mind what she said,' Jonathan snapped. The very mention of her name had his pulses jerking worse than a rodeo bull. 'What's all this about fractions?'

'She's the best teacher ever,' Jamie enthused.

Jonathan looked blank. 'Teacher?'

Patiently Jamie explained. 'Miss Boyd helped me with my maths. I'm going to get all my sums right when I go back to school and I can't wait to see Old Bucky's face. He'll just about turn into a toad!'

He slid past the motor cycle and hurried up the drive, yelling happily over his shoulder, 'I hope Nibby's kept me my flapjacks . . . '

When he was out of earshot Jonathan uttered a short, sharp word which did little to relieve his feelings. To think that Jamie had been visiting the very woman he had decided to keep away from! The child was emotionally vulnerable at the moment and needed a mother figure. It would be disastrous for him to go forming some kind of an attachment to the likes of Miss Boyd.

Volcano-like, sudden fury erupted in his chest. Jonathan didn't bother to examine why as he took off down the road.

# 3

Marissa's heart rate went into overdrive when she heard the forceful banging at her front door. She placed Tippy's food on the floor and rinsed her hands at the sink before hurrying to answer the summons.

One look at the irate man on her doorstep made her go pale. It was the crazy man who had scared her out of her wits last night, and he was obviously keen to make a habit of it. He was glowering like a cornered stag getting ready to fight for his life.

'Good afternoon, Mr Gray,' she managed calmly, 'what can I do for you?'

There was a moment's strained silence while he flicked her with his blue glance. Was she imagining it or had she seen a momentary admiration in his eyes?

Jonathan's stare had indeed softened.

Miss Boyd looked adorable with that dark, glossy curtain of hair framing her delicate features. Her wide green eyes were even wider with apprehension — as they well they might be, he reflected ruefully.

Then he remembered the reason for his visit and grimly returned to the attack.

'I would be obliged if you would stay well away from us,' he grated, realising as he said it just how off he must sound.

Marissa's pretty mouth dropped open. 'I beg your pardon?'

Jonathan ignored the tide of red he could feel rising beneath his collar.

'Keep away from us,' he repeated forcefully, feeling like an utter jerk. 'We want nothing to do with you, is that clear?'

She blinked. 'As mud.'

Jonathan ground his teeth. 'Surely I can't make it any clearer? I want you to stop teaching my nephew mathematics and enticing him here with your chocolate chip cookies.'

Marissa's mouth dropped open. 'You . . . you're Jamie's uncle? You live at Dargle Park?' This, then, was the unpleasant neighbour who had been trying to get grandfather to part with the cottage. She might have known!

'Guilty as charged,' he grated, 'and I shall be warning him to stay away from Rose Cottage in future. It is completely unacceptable that a woman like you be allowed access to my nephew. You're nothing but trouble.'

Marissa couldn't believe what she was hearing. His verbal attack was both unreasonable and insulting.

Unused to being spoken to in this fashion, Marissa looked him up and down much as though he were a cockroach in some slimy alley.

'Aren't you men charming when you wish to be?' she asked sweetly, and slammed the door.

It was Jonathan's turn to blink. He took a deep breath and turned away.

★  ★  ★

Marissa drove to the hospital in Pietermaritzburg that evening to visit her grandfather. He was heavily sedated and unable to converse with her, but his eyes smiled a welcome.

'I've given up my job in Durban, Grandfather,' she told him, taking one of his blue-veined hands in her own. 'I've moved into Rose Cottage. You're not to worry about a thing, d'you hear? In no time you'll be fit again and when you come out of hospital we'll take care of each other. Just concentrate on getting better.'

He nodded weakly and squeezed her hand.

She added in a hearty voice, 'You've always been a fighter, Grandfather. You can't let us down now . . . I'm relying on you.'

Marissa rose early the following morning. Today was the day she intended to set up her pottery studio in the garage, and she couldn't wait to get started. There would be a lot to do, of course. The concrete floor would have to be scrubbed, the walls whitewashed and the improvised shelving firmly secured in place.

Enumerating the items she wanted to sell, she ticked them off on her fingers as she took her mug of redbush tea into the garage.

'Bowls, plates, vases, ginger jars, mugs, ash trays . . . '

Grandfather's old workbench and cupboard were standing in the corner and they would serve very well for her various items of equipment; brushes, sieves, meshes, buckets and airtight jars of damp clay. Once these items were in place she would set up her beloved electric wheel and kiln.

'By tomorrow I should be able to start throwing pots,' she informed Tippy who had followed her from the house and was busy inspecting a clump of catmint growing near the door. 'In the next few weeks I must produce enough things to sell for the Christmas tourist trade.'

'I'll help you, Miss Boyd,' Jamie's

voice piped up behind her.

Marissa spun around in dismay. She'd been very firmly warned off having any further contact with the child, and here he was on her doorstep once again.

'Oh, hello, Jamie.'

She put her mug down on the windowsill and said carefully, 'Look, I'd love you to help me, but I don't think your uncle would approve of your spending so much time here.'

Jamie's gaze was guileless. 'Oh, that's all right, Miss Boyd. He doesn't know I'm here. He's not at Dargle Park this morning 'cause he had to drive to Durban to the airport to fetch my mother. She phoned last night to say she was coming, and it made Uncle Jonathan rather grumpy. I can always tell when he's cross because his face goes blank.

'Did you not want to go along for the ride, Jamie?'

'Uncle Jonathan didn't want me to go. He said he needed to talk to my mother privately and I told him that's fine by me because I'd be bored, anyway. All my mother can talk about are dresses and shoes and what colour she could dye her hair next.'

Marissa murmured in sympathy. 'Ladies love to dress up, don't they? I'm sure your mother will be glad to see you again.'

She was disconcerted to see Jamie shake his head. 'No, she won't.'

Nonplussed, Marissa tried once more to send him away. 'Hadn't you better go home and wait for her?'

Jamie's small chin jutted in defiance. 'No. I don't want to go home, Miss Boyd, I want to stay here and help you. 'Sides, my mother won't be here for hours and hours 'cause Durban's a long way away.'

Marissa hesitated. 'Well . . . '

'I'd like to help you make egg cups, Miss Boyd,' Jamie begged. 'I've never made egg cups before.' His blue eyes were alight with interest.

Marissa hesitated no longer. What the

eye didn't see, the heart didn't grieve. If Jamie's crazy uncle didn't know what he was up to then he couldn't very well complain, could he?

The decision made, all Marissa's teaching instincts surfaced. Children needed a positive outlet for their energies and it would give her great pleasure to develop any creative abilities he might have. She sensed that he wasn't entirely happy at his school, and if she could show him how to mould and glaze things, the sense of achievement might help him to gain more confidence in his own abilities.

'I'd be grateful for your help, Jamie,' she smiled, 'but we won't be making egg cups today because we have to set up the studio first.'

Quickly she explained what needed to be done, and glanced at her watch. 'You can help me until lunchtime and then you'd better run along home. Your mother will become anxious if you're not home when she arrives.'

'No, she won't,' Jamie repeated

matter-of-factly. 'But I'll go home for lunch, just the same. Agnes is making sausages and I like sausages.'

He picked up the broom and took charge of the operation much as if he were the man of the house and she the helpless little woman.

★  ★  ★

Curbing his rising impatience, Jonathan waited in the airport terminal for Nerina to emerge. The woman would doubtless have half a dozen suitcases in tow even though she was only staying for a few days. On past showing it would be a fraught few days, too, filled with demands for his attention, complaints about his household staff, whinges about the food and endless comments about her looks. The incessant, mindless chatter would drive him mad but he could always escape to his study.

'Jonathan, darling,' she cooed, clutching his arm as though it were a lifeline, 'how perfectly lovely to see you again.'

'Hello, Nerina.' And you're a darned liar, he thought as he gave her a dutiful peck on the cheek.

Over her shoulder he noted a bronzed, bored-looking young man glowering at him from beneath a red baseball cap. The man's oversized biceps bulged beneath a black T-shirt.

Jonathan was about to ignore him when Nerina said airily, 'This is Marlin Conrad, Jonathan. He helped me with my luggage at the carousel. Poor little me, I couldn't really be expected to manage all that stuff on my own, could I?' She gave a tinkling laugh. 'Isn't he a perfect charmbag?'

The bag of charm looked positively sulky. Jonathan acknowledged him with a cool nod and reached for the luggage trolley.

'Just a moment, darling. I'm dying for a cigarette and I've run out. Fetch me a packet from the kiosk, will you?' Nerina begged prettily.

As soon as he was out of earshot she

rounded on the man.

'Don't look so cross, Marlin,' she hissed, 'you'll draw unnecessary attention to yourself.'

She stepped closer, her scarlet fingertips stroking his beefy forearm. 'And don't forget, sweetie, you're not to contact me while I'm at Dargle Park. Stay put at The Haven and I'll come to you as soon as I can. Don't worry, it's a decent place; there'll be plenty of food and booze.'

He gave her a petulant stare. 'I'm not used to being a kept man, Nerina. I like to make my own arrangements.'

'I know, darling, but it's only for a week at the most and then we can take up where we left off. I'll make it up to you, I promise. If we play our cards right I'll soon be a rich woman and then we can both do as we like.'

He scowled. 'You'd better deliver, Nerina, or I'll cut you out. I have my own future to think of.'

'Oh, I'll deliver all right, Marlin; I'll have Jonathan's money and I'll get you the cottage, no problem. I want a piece of your pie too. I'm the one with all the contacts, remember? I have plenty of rich friends who own fancy cars and I make it my business to cultivate them.'

'Yes, but it's my boys who do all the dirty work. If I move the operation down here I'll have to find a few locals to work the Durban and Pietermaritzburg areas. That might not be so easy at first.'

'Well, you yourself said it's getting too hot for you in Johannesburg what with the cops nosing around. It makes much more sense to work from a country backwater. As for Jonathan, he's easy meat. I can manipulate him any way I want because he's so besotted with the child. Once we're married I'll drain him dry and you can move into Rose Cottage and we can continue to operate from there . . . in between my flitting off to make more contacts, of course! I'll start cultivating a few fools in Durban, too.'

Marlin smirked. 'Yeah. As you say, we

need somewhere out of the way. You're sure you can get me the place?'

'Like I said, no problem, darling boy. I have ways and means. The stupid old man who lives at Rose Cottage won't take much persuading. He looked positively terrified when I told him I'd get the place in the end.'

Her red mouth twisted into a nasty smile.

'As Jonathan's wife I'll have both money and influence and if that doesn't work then I'm sure you'll be able to arrange something unfortunate for him, Marlin. He might even settle for a bribe. Money talks, you know, and I'll have a whole bagful, courtesy of my unsuspecting, absent-minded husband.'

The nasty smile gave way to a happy sigh. 'Jonathan is such a geek.'

'Yeah. Looks it, too. What did you say he does all day?'

'I don't rightly know. He sits at the computer typing letters or something.'

'Well, as long as he keeps his nose out of our business . . . '

She giggled. 'Our illegal activities, you mean.'

'Shut up,' Marlin snapped, 'here he comes.'

Nerina snatched the packet of cigarettes and gazed adoringly into Jonathan's face.

She was an attractive woman in a brassy sort of way, with large, blue eyes and a highlighted mane of hair which feathered her shoulders in an artfully tousled manner. Unfortunately she insisted on covering her arms with numerous gold bracelets which jangled, and he detested bracelets which jangled.

'How are things, Nerina?' he enquired politely in the car; a mistake, because she spent the following thirty minutes talking about herself.

Deliberately he changed the subject. 'Your son is home for the school holidays, as I mentioned.'

'Oh, drat. I was hoping we'd be able to spend some time alone together, Jonathan. I've come all this way to see you.'

'I would have thought it was in order to see Jamie,' he drawled. 'He's having some difficulty settling in at his new school, like I said.'

She tossed her blonde tresses. 'Take no notice, darling, he's just playing up.'

Jonathan's jaw tightened. Did the woman have no compassion? She was so wrapped up in herself she had no time even for her own flesh and blood.

'He is asking if he may live with me at Dargle Park and attend the local primary school in Howick. I think it may be a possibility. It's a good school.'

She shrugged. 'Whatever. I can't be bothered with all the ins and outs. I have my career to focus on at the moment. Fashion photography is my life, you know.'

'Sure it is,' he agreed dryly.

She tossed him a sly glance. 'I have been offered a very lucrative contract in Paris and I'm keen to take it.'

Jonathan said nothing. Here it comes, he thought.

'It will mean,' she added sweetly,

'that you will not have to bother yourself with schooling or any other consideration because I shall take Jamie with me.'

Her meaning was clear.

'Of course,' she stated boldly, 'I would prefer to be known as the mistress of Dargle Park. I could freelance from there and come and go as I like. What could be easier? You would have complete responsibility for my son who appears to adore you, anyway. It's a rather neat answer all round, I believe. How about it?'

Jonathan was under no illusion as to what she really meant. She wanted his money and couldn't wait to get her greedy little hands on it. From time to time she'd appeared at Dargle Park to ask him for loans which he'd generously doled out, knowing full well she'd conveniently forget to repay them. What Nerina didn't realise was that he was no fool; he'd taken measures to safeguard his fortune for Jamie who would one day inherit Dargle Park because it went without saying that there would be no further heirs on the scene.

Once he and Nerina were married he would specify a fixed allowance for her each month and she would be forced to live within her means. Wait until she saw the prenuptial agreement he had in mind, too!

He'd bet his last cent that within months she'd become bored with life at Dargle Park anyway and rush back to Johannesburg, unencumbered with responsibility and determined to continue with her freewheeling, hedonistic lifestyle.

Hiding his disgust, he said smoothly, 'Now that you mention it, Nerina, I feel your suggestion has merit.'

'Of course it has. I was sure you'd see it my way, darling.'

Jonathan's face was expressionless. 'We will get engaged immediately.'

Nerina gasped, unable to believe he'd capitulated so quickly.

'I'd like a large solitaire diamond, Jonathan,' she purred, 'something really impressive. I can't stand piffling little stones. One can't make a statement with them.'

She examined her perfectly manicured hands and suggested avidly, 'Why not stop off in Durban now and buy the ring? I'd like to show if off to all my friends in Howick. Perhaps we could throw a party next week.'

Jonathan steeled himself to reply. 'A good idea,' he nodded, his voice bland. 'I know of a reliable jeweller in West Street . . .'

★　★　★

Marissa glanced at her watch and gasped. 'Heavens, it's almost lunchtime, Jamie. You'd better hurry home before your uncle returns.'

'Oh, Uncle Jonathan probably won't notice if I'm late. He's a professor, you know. Professors are absent-minded.'

Marissa's eyes widened incredulously. 'A professor? I see.' That explained a lot . . . like why he was so nutty. 'Well . . . thank you for your help, Jamie. The walls are looking great.'

'Oh, that's all right, Miss Boyd.'

'You'd better sort your hair out, too. There are one or two spots of paint on top, and don't forget to wash your hands thoroughly.'

'I won't. Can I come back after lunch and help with the shelving?'

'What about your mother?'

'Oh, she won't care what I do.'

'In that case,' she winked conspiratorially, 'play it by ear.'

He grinned back. 'OK, I will. 'Bye, Miss Boyd.'

Marissa watched him hurry up the hill and sighed with relief. He was an endearing child and she would hate him to get into trouble on her account.

As Jamie hurried into the house he couldn't suppress a slight feeling of guilt. Nibby thought he'd been playing in the garden but the truth was he'd slipped away just after she'd given him his morning tea. To make up for his naughtiness he washed his face and hands more thoroughly than usual and presented himself at the dining table with minutes to spare and a fixed smile.

Mrs Nibela eyed him sternly. 'Where have you been all morning?'

Jamie had been taught not to lie. He said simply, 'I was helping the pretty lady I told you about, Nibby . . . the one Uncle Jonathan should marry.'

Mrs Nibela placed his lunch before him and shook her head. 'You're talking nonsense again, Jamie. You must tell the truth. Where have you been?'

'I told you, Nibby. I've been helping her paint the garage walls. I didn't have time to get the paint out of my hair.'

Mrs Nibela's eyes narrowed sharply as she noted the white paint spots. So the child was telling the truth, after all! Who was this woman, then, and where did she live?

'I'm going back after lunch to help her with the shelving, Nibby,' Jamie added through a mouthful of potato.

'Where is this garage?'

'It's at Rose Cottage, just down the road.'

'Aah. Well, I will go with you. I would like to meet this woman. But first,' she told him firmly, 'you will wash your hair.'

If Jamie had found a suitable wife for his uncle then she would need to inspect the woman. Professor Gray would have to make up his mind quickly because that awful Mrs Nerina Gray was coming to stay and anybody could see she had plans to marry the boss.

Mrs Nibela accompanied Jamie down the hill to Rose Cottage and knocked determinedly on the door. Marissa, having just dried the dishes, called out cheerily, 'Come in, Jamie.'

She looked at the large Zulu woman standing on the doorstep and hid her surprise.

'Oh . . . good afternoon.'

Mrs Nibela came straight to the point. 'I am Mrs Rose Nibela, Professor Gray's housekeeper. I have brought Jamie to help you. He is hoping that you will marry his uncle and I have come to see if you are suitable. The professor is a very good man and he must marry a good woman. I have come to see if you are that woman.'

Marissa gaped at her. Recovering herself, she said quickly, 'I am very flattered that Jamie thinks I would make a suitable wife for the professor, but I am not looking for a husband at the moment, Mrs Nibela. You see, I have a business to run. From next week I will be selling pottery goods from my shop in the garage, and I hope that you and your friends will come to view what I have for sale. Jamie has been helping me to set everything up and I'm very grateful to him. He is a wonderful boy.'

Mrs Nibela's face relaxed. 'Yes, I am glad you can see that. Jamie is a good boy, just as the professor is a good man.'

'Would you like a cup of tea?' Marissa offered, desperate to change the subject.

The woman refused politely. 'I will

fetch Jamie later on,' she promised, and took herself off without another word.

Marissa watched her ample back departing up the drive, unable to believe what she'd just heard.

Jamie was eyeing her confidently. 'Mrs Nibela likes you, Miss Boyd. Will you come to tea soon? Agnes makes smashing flapjacks.'

Marissa murmured suitably and ushered him out to the garage. 'Our first job, Jamie, is to dust off the planks . . . '

Before she locked the garage that evening Marissa took one last look around. The shelving was neatly in place along one wall and sported a variety of goods which had been unpacked from their straw-filled boxes and displayed to advantage against the pretty pastel shelf paper.

A pink plastic cloth covered Grandfather's workbench where her brushes and glazes stood, and the wheel and kiln had been connected up, ready for use.

# 4

Jonathan Gray eased the Land Rover into the garage and killed the engine, grateful to be home at last.

He'd spent a trying few hours at the jewellers in Durban where Nerina, always happy to be the centre of attention, had ensured that the entire staff had been kept on the hop. Once the ring had finally been chosen he had taken Nerina for lunch at the prestigious beachfront hotel she'd insisted upon, and after having endured her inane chatter during the long drive home he was heartily sick of her.

Heaven alone knew how he would be able to put up with the woman for a lifetime, for that is what it would take. He was an honourable man and having given his word he would not go back on it. He would do his duty and in the process he would raise a happy, secure little boy. It was the least he could do in his brother's memory.

'Alpheus will bring in the luggage,' he told Nerina politely, ushering her through the front door. 'Mrs Nibela has prepared your room as usual.'

The housekeeper appeared at that moment and greeted Nerina in a restrained manner. She had no time for a woman who had no time for her own son.

'A tray of tea is waiting in the living-room, sir,' she informed Jonathan.

'Tea?' Nerina gave a snigger. 'How tame. I'll have a whisky.'

Jonathan shrugged. 'Suit yourself.'

Mrs Nibela turned politely to Nerina. 'Jamie has had his bath and is waiting to see you, Madam. Shall I send him down?'

'Well yes, I suppose so.'

When she was out of earshot Nerina said crossly, 'Why you keep on that bossy woman is beyond me! When we are married I shall dismiss her.'

Jonathan handed her a glass, his face

bland, concealing sudden rage. 'You will do no such thing,' he said pleasantly. There was a steely note behind the tones which Nerina did not much care for, but it would not do to reveal her irritation. When they were married she would see to it that she got her own way.

'Hello, Mummy,' Jamie greeted her in a wooden little voice. He went to embrace her, but was waved away as though he had some notifiable disease.

'My hair. You'll mess up my hair.'

He looked as though she'd hit him. 'Your hair looks very nice, Mummy,' he choked.

'Yes, it does, doesn't it?' Nerina patted and teased at the blonde strands with her long fingers. 'It's the latest style, you know. I always go for the latest style. My hairdresser said . . . ' she prattled on while Jamie looked bored and his uncle stared fixedly at the opposite wall.

'What have you been doing with yourself today, Jamie?' Jonathan asked, determined to change the subject. 'I'm sure your mother would like to hear about your day.'

Jamie regarded him gravely. 'Well, I helped Miss Boyd to paint her garage wall and then we put up the shelving for the plates and mugs and then we — '

'Miss Boyd?' Jonathan interrupted sharply, clamping down his irritation. It looked as though he would be having another strong word with the stubborn little occupant of Rose Cottage. She had shown a blatant disregard of his wishes. It was doubly galling that his pulse rate had doubled at the very mention of her name.

'She's very pretty, isn't she?' Jamie enthused. He turned shining eyes on his uncle's face. 'You should marry her, Uncle Jonathan. She knows how to make egg cups.'

Nerina's head shot up. 'What nonsense you talk, Jamie! Your uncle is going to marry me and no-one else. See my new ring . . . ' she flashed the large, showy diamond under his nose.

Jamie stared at it uncomprehendingly. 'I don't think that would be a very good idea, Mummy.'

His chin lifted in defiance and added with childish candour, 'Miss Boyd is much nicer than you are; I would prefer Uncle Jonathan to marry Miss Boyd.'

Nerina's perfect complexion became mottled with an unbecoming red. 'Go to your room at once, Jamie,' she said coldly. 'I will hear no more of this Boyd creature!'

Jamie's eyes filled with tears. 'I don't like you very much, Mummy,' he gulped as he ran from the room.

Jonathan, who didn't like Nerina very much either, gave her a cold stare. 'That was a little harsh, wasn't it? The child is entitled to his opinions, Nerina. He meant no harm.'

'He's a brat,' she snapped. 'He's been a trial to me from the day he was born and you are welcome to him.'

'In that case,' Jonathan's voice was

mild but it dared her to argue, 'you will have no objection to my formally adopting him.'

'None whatsoever.'

He kept his voice casual. 'It might be an idea to set things in motion straight away. I'll speak to my solicitor tomorrow.'

Nerina shot him a sly look from under her lashes. 'Whatever you say, darling.' He really did mean to marry her, then! She could hardly wait to tell Marlin.

'I want complete custody of Jamie, Nerina. After all, you'll be away at work half the time. It would make sense, should anything happen to you.'

'Oh, definitely. I'll drink to that.'

Hiding his relief, Jonathan got up to pour her another whisky.

★　★　★

Tippy's kittens arrived a few days later. There were only two of them and they both resembled Tiger.

'Well, never mind that,' Marissa consoled her, 'at least they're healthy, and we can't all be as beautiful as our mothers, you know.'

She transferred the little family into a shallow cardboard box and placed it near the door so that Tippy could nip outside when she wanted to.

A wistful little thought struck her: she would love to be a mother too. At twenty-seven her clock was ticking. But it would entail meeting the right man first; something she had as yet failed to do.

'If I ever have a son, Tippy,' she remarked dreamily, 'he must be just like Jamie.' Her husband, naturally, would be a man like Brett Morgan of the Ace Detective Agency . . .

Jamie visited her briefly during the afternoon and was delighted with the kittens. Marissa promised to consider giving him one when they were older, and he went away on cloud nine.

★   ★   ★

On Friday after breakfast was over and the cottage had been tidied, Marissa telephoned the hospital, just as she had done each morning during the week. She was overjoyed to hear that her grandfather had rallied, as she knew he would.

She went into the garage to prepare a lump of clay in readiness for when Jamie arrived. Together they would mould the promised egg cups which hopefully would be glazed and ready for use by the time he returned to school on Sunday afternoon. When he still hadn't arrived by mid morning she assumed he'd forgotten their arrangement.

Without giving it another thought she sat down at the wheel and proceeded with her own work; a salad bowl she'd designed in her head while in the bath the previous evening. She intended to incise on it the same pattern as the one on the small blue bowls already displayed on the shelf. It would make a complete set; the perfect gift for some discerning hostess.

Meanwhile, Jamie lay listlessly on the sofa in the living-room. 'My head hurts, Mummy, and I've got a sore throat,' he croaked.

'Go and play, Jamie, I can't be bothered with your whining,' his mother snapped, returning to her magazine.

Two large tears spilled from his blue eyes. Unable to help it, he gave a great sniff.

'You can stop snivelling! Have you packed your things for school? You can't expect me to do it for you.'

'I'll do it now, Mummy.'

Slowly he heaved himself from the sofa and took himself upstairs to his room where Mrs Nibela found him half-an-hour later, muttering incoherently, his face alarmingly flushed. She immediately went to inform the professor.

Jonathan looked up from his computer and sighed. At this rate he'd never finish chapter five and he had a deadline for his publisher. Brett Morgan would have to come up with something brilliant in the next few hours . . .

'What is it, Mrs Nibela?'

'Jamie is ill. You had better come and see him, sir.'

'Have you told his mother?'

'No, sir. Mrs Gray is busy on the telephone. She has been speaking for the past twenty-five minutes and I did not like to interrupt her.'

Jonathan bounded up the stairs two at a time and opened the bedroom door. 'Not feeling well, old son?' he asked casually.

'Sore throat,' Jamie croaked feverishly.

Gently Jonathan removed his shoes and helped him into bed. 'We'll send for Doctor McKenzie and he'll sort you out in no time. Mrs Nibela, see that he is comfortable and bring a glass of water, will you?'

In the hall Nerina was still speaking on the telephone. Jonathan, a tolerant man, found that his patience had worn thin.

'I'm sorry, Nerina,' he interrupted her firmly; 'I must use the telephone at once.'

She muttered crossly into the mouthpiece before slamming it into the cradle, her blue eyes flashing in outrage.

'I do not appreciate being interrupted like this, Jonathan.'

'Too bad, my dear,' he clipped. 'Your son needs medical attention.'

'Nonsense. He's playing up because he doesn't want to go back to school.'

She snatched the keys of Jonathan's silver Mercedes from their nook in the hall and announced defiantly, 'I'll be having lunch in Howick today. There are some matters I must see to . . . ' and flounced out the door.

Marissa had just placed the salad bowl on the workbench to 'rest' in between stages when she heard tyres screeching to a halt outside the front gate. She removed her work apron and hurried into the kitchen to wash her hands before answering the impatient ringing of the doorbell. One look at the haughty blonde standing on the door-step told her the woman meant trouble.

'Can I help you?' she asked, hoping this wasn't a prospective customer who had been driving past. The shop wasn't really open for business yet. She needed another week or two to build up her stock.

Nerina Gray looked her up and down from narrowed eyes and lost no time in making her demands.

'I'm looking for the old man who lives here. Be good enough to call him; I haven't all day.'

Marissa was taken aback at such rudeness. 'May I know your name?'

'I'm Mrs Nerina Gray from Dargle Park. Hurry up, please.'

This obnoxious woman, then, was Jamie's mother. No wonder he didn't like her very much! And she was going to marry the professor who was equally obnoxious. Well, they deserved each another!

'I take it you mean my grandfather, Mrs Gray. He's not here at present.'

'When will he be back?'

'I'm not sure. He's in the hospital.'

Nerina frowned. 'Which hospital? I shall have to look him up because I must speak with him immediately. What's his name?'

Marissa had no intention of obliging. 'I will not tell you that, Mrs Gray,' she said politely but firmly. 'He is in no condition to receive visitors at present. Anything you have to say must be said to me since I am now living here with him. What is it in connection with?'

Nerina's cheeks fired angrily. 'Snooty piece, aren't you? I wish to make your grandfather a further proposition concerning our last conversation in which I told him I intended to purchase this cottage.'

Marissa's pretty mouth tightened. Who did the Grays think they were, demanding this and demanding that?

'Rose Cottage is not for sale,' she retorted crisply. 'Goodbye, Mrs Gray.'

She closed the door smartly, but not before catching sight of the large diamond ring on Nerina's finger.

'Showy and vulgar,' she told Tippy disapprovingly, 'even though it must have cost him a packet.'

*  ★  ★

Marissa was much encouraged by her grandfather's recovery when she visited him that evening. His eyes were bright and his handclasp almost as firm as it used to be. In the few days since she'd last seen him he appeared to have taken on a new lease of life.

'I'm glad you're here to stay, Marissa,' he told her simply. 'It's given me a new purpose, love. I'm determined to recover fully.'

'And you will, Grandfather. When you come out of here we have a lot of living to do. All you have to do is rest and persevere with the drug therapy and your heart rhythms will soon be normal.'

Chatting calmly, she told him about Tippy's kittens and the new business and how Jamie had helped her with the garage, to all of which he nodded and smiled. Then unwilling to tire him, she rose to leave.

He raised a blue-veined hand. 'There's something I want you to do for me, Marissa.'

'Sure, Grandfather.'

'It would relive me greatly if I could speak to my neighbour, Jonathan Gray, about my investment portfolio. He's good with stocks and shares, you know, and I rely on his advice. Take a walk up to Dargle Park and ask him to pay me a visit, will you?'

Marissa's heart sank. The thought of paying a visit to the cranky Gray household held not the slightest appeal, but she couldn't very well refuse the old man's request. At least he was taking an interest in life again.

As a retired headmaster he wasn't a wealthy man, but had nevertheless made careful investments with his capital. At all costs he must be kept from worrying about them.

'No problem,' she smiled, 'I'll go first thing in the morning.'

★  ★  ★

Mrs Nibela answered the door, her black eyes round with curiosity. It was the young woman from Rose Cottage.

When Marissa offered her the traditional Zulu greeting of 'Sanibona', her face broke into a broad smile.

'Good morning, Miss Boyd. You have come to see the boy?'

'Jamie? Why, no. I've come to speak to Professor Gray.'

Mrs Nibela's smile widened further so that her teeth flashed whitely in her black face.

'You wish to see the professor? That is good. Very good. Come with me.'

If her employer would open his eyes for one minute he would see that this was a quality young woman. Besides, Jamie liked her.

At her knock Jonathan barked a command to enter. 'A young lady to see you, sir,' Mrs Nibela informed him smugly, and withdrew.

A curious expression crossed Jonathan's face; quickly replaced by a blank mask. He stood up slowly, his eyes strangely intent.

'What can I do for you, Miss Boyd?'

Oh help, Marissa thought as she advanced into the room. The professor may be impossibly loony but he was the most attractive man she'd ever seen. A girl could drown in those blue, darkly lashed eyes, especially when they were looking at her as though she were the most important thing in the world. And as for that gorgeous dark hair of his . . .

Stop staring, she commanded herself silently. Her heart was making like a Mexican jumping bean so that the words were locked in her throat. If only she could get a few of them out . . .

Jonathan was staring back at her, his gaze filled with wholly masculine interest as he noted the neat, sleeveless blouse and faded denim skirt. Her clothes were hardly the height of fashion, with those worn leather sandals and matching belt clasping her slim waist, but then she was the type of female who could wear anything and look stunning.

'I've come with a message from my grandfather . . . ' Marissa began huskily.

'A cup of coffee?' Jonathan offered quickly, surprised at himself. This would not be a social visit and the last thing he needed was to prolong it. He didn't want any distractions in the shape of Marissa Boyd just when Brett Morgan was getting ready to kiss the beautiful spy in red . . .

Without waiting for Marissa's reply he went to the door and called down the passage. 'Two coffees please, Mrs Nibela.'

Mrs Nibela was one step ahead of him. She'd already ordered Agnes to butter a plate of scones and was busy assembling a tray using the Georgian silver coffee pot and antique cups the professor's mother had kept for special occasions.

Jonathan noted the pot and the cups and shot her an enquiring glance.

'Enjoy your coffee, sir,' Mrs Nibela said blandly and closed the door behind her with a happy sigh. Hopefully when the young lady saw the silver pot she would be impressed. The professor was a rich man, but also one of impeccable taste. Any woman would be proud to marry him.

Jonathan cleared his throat. This was bound to be awkward. The last time he'd set eyes on Miss Boyd he'd behaved like a fool, but now that he was safely engaged to Nerina it would do no harm to try and make amends. In the interests of his friendship with her grandfather, of course.

'Milk and sugar?' he enquired politely.

Marissa was equally polite. 'Thank you.'

She bit into a scone and eyed him warily. This red carpet treatment was not what she'd expected. For some reason he was concealing his dislike of her beneath perfect manners. Well, she would do the same.

'Lovely weather we're having,' she remarked pleasantly, polishing off the last of the delicious scone. The professor's cook obviously knew her job.

Jonathan's mouth twitched. 'Indeed it is.'

'Your garden is looking magnificent.'

'Is it? I hadn't noticed, but that's because I usually have my nose in a book,' he said ruefully.

She looked a little shocked. 'In that case you should take a walk outside. It's a beautiful day and there are all those bougainvillea bushes, and the poinsettia just coming into flower, and those incredible Iceberg roses along the fence . . . '

'Is that what they are?'

He seemed abstracted. His eyes were boring right through her, just as though she wasn't there. It was disconcerting.

When his gaze fastened on her mouth, it suddenly sharpened.

'Look, I don't want to keep you because you're obviously a busy man,' she said hastily, 'but I've come to ask you if — '

'More coffee?' Jonathan enquired absently. He was thinking about how he would describe the lips of that spy in red. Soft and luscious, just like Miss Boyd's . . .

'No thank you. My grandfather — '

'When last did you see Brett?'

Marissa's mouth dropped open. 'Who?'

Jonathan affected surprise. 'Your fiancé, Brett Morgan. When last did you see him?'

She blushed scarlet. 'Oh, that Brett . . . '

Basically an honest girl, she had to admit she'd been frightened into lying the other evening and it now behoved her to put the record straight. There was no point in perpetuating a deceit. Marissa hated deceit.

She swallowed. 'To be honest, we . . .

er, I am no longer engaged,' she mumbled.

'You were dumped?'

'Certainly not! What girl worth her salt would allow herself to be dumped? It was by mutual agreement.' It was an improvisation on the spur of the moment, but a girl had her pride to consider.

'I'm relieved to hear it. A private investigator is not a good proposition, Miss Boyd. Unlikely husband material, I would think. He'd always be running off on some adventure or other, leaving no time for the family.'

Quite unable to resist it, Marissa rallied hotly to her hero's defence.

'Oh, but you're wrong! Brett Morgan is a marvellous, caring man who would do anything for the woman he loved. He'd make a stunning father, too. You have no idea how wonderful he is.'

Jonathan sipped his coffee and hid his delight beneath a casual manner. 'I have a fair idea,' he said softly, his eyes gleaming with secret amusement.

'It's just that . . . well, we decided not to get married after all,' Marissa finished lamely. She was beginning to feel uncomfortable. Why was he so interested in her affairs? She wished she hadn't opened her mouth so wide in the first place.

Firmly she changed the subject. 'My grandfather asked me to come and see you. He wonders if you would be so kind as to visit him in St Anne's hospital? He needs some financial advice.'

'I would be delighted. Is he well enough to receive visitors?'

'Within reason. He's rallied remarkably well and the doctor is very pleased. If all goes well he should be home again in a couple of weeks.'

'That's wonderful news.'

Marissa stood up to go. Jonathan moved swiftly to open the door. Almost as if he couldn't wait to get rid of her, she thought crossly. Being a tall girl herself, she nevertheless had to look up at him as she thanked him for the coffee.

He gave a sudden smile which sent an attractive crease down his tanned cheeks and made his incredible eyes seem even bluer.

Marissa caught her breath. He looked quite different when he smiled. It turned him into a man she would like to get to know better; a man with tough, handsome features and oddly compassionate eyes. It was the face of a man to be trusted. Why hadn't she noticed it before?

He ushered her through the front door and into the garden with the intention of seeing her all the way to the gate. Marissa sought frantically for something to say.

'Like I said, your garden is very beautiful.'

Jonathan's gaze dropped to her soft, pink mouth. 'Very,' he murmured. 'Goodbye, Miss Boyd.'

On a crazy impulse, one he knew he would regret later, he bent and kissed that mouth. It was something he'd wanted to do ever since he'd met her.

Nerina, observing him from the living-room window, flew into a rage. 'It's that hoity-toity woman from Rose Cottage,' she spat. 'How dare she come up to Dargle Park and try to take Jonathan from me? I'll get Marlin to sort her out!'

'I beg your pardon, Madam?' Mrs Nibela asked innocently. She collected up Nerina's tea things and paused. 'Did you say something?'

'Shut up and mind your own business,' Nerina grated. She flashed her ring under the housekeeper's nose. 'I shall marry the professor by Christmas, you stupid woman, and when I am mistress here you will be the first one to go.'

'Yes, Madam,' Mrs Nibela agreed imperturbably.

She returned to the kitchen in a highly optimistic mood knowing full well that she was part of the furniture at Dargle Park. The professor would never allow her to be dismissed. It was Mrs Gray who would be the one to go and then the boss would marry the suitable Miss Boyd whom Jamie liked. She, Rose Nibela, felt it in her very bones.

So confident was Mrs Nibela of her predictions that she sailed into the kitchen and informed a startled Agnes, 'You will be baking a wedding cake before long, my good girl. It won't be for the Madam, either.'

# 5

It was a warm and peaceful country morning with the doves cooing in the acacia trees and the bees buzzing in the pink cosmos beside the road. Marissa noticed none of these as she walked home, her thoughts in a fine state of confusion.

The professor ate his lunch in rather more abstraction than usual. He hated to admit it but he was bowled over by Marissa Boyd, so much so that he'd allowed his habitual self control to slip. It had been a mistake to kiss her because that one kiss hadn't been enough.

He looked up from his salad to find Nerina's eyes fastened narrowly on him.

'You had a visitor this morning?' she queried sweetly.

'Yes. Miss Boyd from Rose Cottage.'

'What did she want?'

'She asked me to visit her grandfather. He's in the hospital.'

'Ah.' Her gaze became thoughtful. 'His name is . . . ?'

'Tom Boyd.'

'Which hospital, darling?'

'St Anne's, I believe. Why are you so interested, Nerina?'

She gave a sympathetic smile. 'I think I'll send an arrangement of flowers. It would be a neighbourly gesture, don't you think?'

He stared at her in surprise. 'Yes, it would. Thank you, Nerina.'

★   ★   ★

Nerina drove out to The Haven Inn and found Marlin Conrad in a state of extreme boredom.

'I am getting fed up with waiting, Nerina,' he told her sourly. 'There is nothing to do in this dump. You said we'd only be here for a week and now you're saying we must stay for two. I want to get back to Johannesburg where there are a few nightclubs.'

'Patience, darling. We must keep the end result in view, must we not? I will be a rich woman soon.'

'How soon?'

'Well, I'm working on it. I've told Jonathan I intend to be married by Christmas, which is only a few weeks away. With my husband's money I shall secure Rose Cottage and you can start moving your equipment down from Johannesburg. I've had a look at the garage; it's a double, with space for a workshop as well and I think it will be big enough. I mean, you only have to do one BMW at a time, don't you? It doesn't need much space to spray one car and change the number plates.'

'It's not that simple, Nerina. I have to file off the engine number and stamp on new one. I intend to expand the operation too . . . I'm keen on doing Mercs as well. There's a growing market for stolen cars of every description, but especially Mercs.'

He gave a sudden grin. 'We might even arrange to 'steal' your husband's Merc, Nerina. It would be a piece of cake. You can tell me where and when, and when the deed's done you can collect the insurance money.'

'We'll decide on all that when the time comes. In the meantime we need to secure the property.'

She frowned. 'We have a slight problem, though. The old man is in hospital and the granddaughter has moved in. I sounded her out, but she won't play ball so I intend to visit the old man this afternoon and see how the land lies. If they are not prepared to cooperate then you can go ahead and arrange something nasty.'

He chuckled. 'It will be a pleasure, Nerina. I'm very creative when it comes to that sort of thing. It will give me something to occupy my thoughts.'

They ate lunch together in the dining-room of The Haven and afterwards sat drinking numerous cups of coffee until it was time for Nerina to visit the hospital.

After tapping briskly on Tom Boyd's door she flung it open.

'Oh . . . '

Her eyes widened in shock as she stared at the man seated at Tom Boyd's bedside.

'Hello, Nerina,' Jonathan greeted her, equally surprised. He got up to find her another chair. 'You really did mean it, then. Where are the flowers?'

She recovered herself swiftly. 'Oh, you mean about being a good neighbour? Of course I meant it, only I didn't have time to visit the florist.'

She turned sweetly to the elderly man lying in the bed.

'How are you doing, Mr Boyd?'

Marissa's grandfather stared at her in disbelief. This was the unpleasant young woman who had visited him a few weeks back and demanded that he sell her his home!

'I'm recovering well,' he said stiffly. What the dickens was she doing here? He could hardly believe that she was a friend of Jonathan's. 'I recall having met you,' he continued, 'but I don't remember your name.'

Nerina smiled brilliantly. 'I'm Jonathan's fiancée, Nerina. We hope to be married by Christmas.'

Tom Boyd's gaze locked with Jonathan's. 'Is this true?'

'Yes,' Jonathan said shortly, and looked away.

'Then . . . I wish you every happiness.'

Suddenly weary, Tom Boyd closed his eyes. Surely Jonathan had more sense than to shackle himself to a shrew like that? The man was making a huge mistake, even he could see that.

Jonathan stood up. 'You need to rest now, Tom, so I'll visit you tomorrow and we can discuss your portfolio then. In the meantime I'll do a spot of research and hopefully come back with some good news.'

Tom nodded his thanks.

'Let's go, Nerina.'

'You go on, darling. I'll see you at

home. I must do some shopping while I'm in town.'

'Where are you parked? I'll walk you to the car.'

'No need. You go on home.'

Jonathan nodded, shook Tom's hand and departed, unaware that Nerina was waiting to pounce. As soon as he was out of earshot she turned back to the bed, her sugary manner replaced by one of determined ruthlessness.

'Mr Boyd, you will remember that we had a little chat concerning Rose Cottage? You would do well to reconsider my offer. Jonathan is keen to return the cottage to the estate, but is unwilling to take a hard line because of his friendship with you. I am not so foolish. I must warn you that as his future wife I will not allow sentiment to stand in the way . . . I intend to give him the cottage as a wedding present and I will instruct the agent in Howick to bring you the documents to sign as soon as you are able. Is that clear?'

She gave him a hard glance and

picked up her handbag.

'Remember what I have said! It will be in your interests to comply, Mr Boyd, or we may be forced to take stronger measures. Good day.'

When she'd gone the old man reached for his bell and pressed the buzzer. Suddenly he wasn't feeling very well . . .

\*     \*     \*

Jonathan drove home thoughtfully, in no way deceived as to Nerina's sudden generosity of spirit. She was up to something and he would make it his business to find out what it was. He wasn't quite the fool she thought he was . . .

On reaching Dargle Park he immediately went up to Jamie's bedroom to entertain him for the remainder of the afternoon. With a mother like that Jamie needed all the attention he could get.

He'd lost no time in discussing the

adoption process with his solicitor on the telephone and intended to expedite the matter as soon as possible. It would ease his mind considerably to know that he had full parental rights, but if only things were different he'd have chosen to marry someone who loved children . . . someone like Marissa Boyd.

Jamie was sitting up in bed. He looked pale as he fiddled listlessly with a piece of Lego, obviously bored with life.

'I hate everything,' he whined peevishly as soon as he saw his uncle. 'I even hate sausages.'

'It's only because you're still feeling a little unwell, Jamie. In no time you'll be back at school playing with your friends.'

'No, I won't. I hate school. I'm not going back.'

Jonathan sighed. 'Look, old son, we'll discuss it later. Right now I'm going to read you a story.'

'I don't feel like a story.'

'A video, then? I'll fetch the small television set from the guest bedroom.'

'No, I want to make egg cups,' Jamie croaked.

Jonathan frowned. 'I'm afraid I can't show you how to make egg cups, Jonathan.'

'Miss Boyd can make egg cups and she said she'd teach me. Uncle Jonathan, please phone Miss Boyd and ask her to come here and teach me how to make egg cups.'

'Jamie . . . '

'I really, really want Miss Boyd to come and teach me how to make egg cups,' Jamie insisted. 'Uncle Jonathan, please phone Miss Boyd and ask her to — '

'All right, all right, I'll phone Miss Boyd.'

Jonathan raked a hand through his hair. 'It's too late for her to visit now but I'll invite her to come up to Dargle Park tomorrow morning if she's not too busy. Will that do?'

Jamie brightened. 'All right. I'll have

that story now, please. The one where the pirate king smuggled all that con . . . con . . . '

'Contraband?'

'Yes, and hid it in that cave where the skeleton was.'

'Right. The pirate king it is.'

Jonathan went to the bookshelf to locate the book in question and Jamie, watching him, gave a great sigh. Miss Boyd would soon be coming to see him and suddenly the world was not such a bad place after all. He even felt hungry again.

'Will you ask Agnes to cook some sausages for my dinner, please . . . ?'

★　★　★

By the time Mrs Nibela went to announce that dinner was ready that evening, the sky outside had darkened to pewter and fierce wind was wreaking havoc in the garden. Great thunderheads rolled across the heavens, heavy with the promise of rain.

Jonathan seated Nerina at the polished mahogany table as the first crashes of thunder sounded, having been preceded by bolts of lightning so bright that they illuminated the distant mountains.

He and Nerina had very little in common and when they were alone the conversation was 'heavy weather'. It was an apt analogy, Jonathan reflected wryly, given the fury of the elements outside.

'A tropical storm at its best,' he remarked, searching for something to say. 'Or if you like, nature at its most ferocious. It's breathtaking, isn't it?'

Nerina looked sour. 'I'm not impressed.'

She drank her mushroom soup uneasily and asked, 'How long will this last?'

'Oh, an hour or so, and then we'll have pelting rain all night. The garden with be wrecked.'

She glanced at him suspiciously. 'Since when have you been interested in the garden?'

Since Miss Boyd had pointed out to him that it was beautiful, to be honest. He'd taken a good look at the flowering shrubs when he'd walked back from seeing her to the gate and had been suitably impressed. They were every bit as lovely as she'd said.

'Are you interested in gardening, Nerina?' he enquired smoothly, placing the conversational ball in her court. 'I trust that you will take it upon yourself to supervise Alpheus when we are married; not that he needs much instruction. He's an excellent worker.'

'Me? Heavens no, I'd be bored out of my skull, Jonathan.' She didn't bother to hide her irritation. 'I have no intention of allowing my hands to become wrecked by the soil. My manicurist in Johannesburg says . . . '

She droned on until Jonathan, unable to bear another word, signalled her to stop. The noise overhead was frightful, and once or twice the lights dipped. By the time they had finished their desert, the electricity supply gave out completely, plunging the house into darkness.

Nerina gave a small shriek. 'Do something, Jonathan. I hate country living! This would never happen in Johannesburg.'

'Then you will have to get used to it, won't you, my dear?' he replied blandly. 'I'll see if I can find some candles.'

'On seconds thoughts, don't bother. I'm going to bed. I can't stand this sort of thing, it's so uncivilised.'

He shrugged. 'Suit yourself.'

Mrs Nibela had found a box of candles in the pantry and was busy setting them up around the house. 'Jamie is already asleep,' she told Jonathan, 'but I will take one or two upstairs for the Madam.'

'Thank you, Mrs Nibela. Goodnight.'

'Goodnight, sir.'

As Jonathan went into the study he remembered that he hadn't yet telephoned Miss Boyd about her visit to Jamie. He picked up the receiver and frowned. The line was dead.

Thoughtfully he raked a hand through his hair. He'd be compelled to drive down to Rose Cottage and ask her in person, or Jamie would be very disappointed. It would relieve his mind, too, to know that she was all right. Like Nerina, Marissa used to live in a city. Perhaps she could use a few candles . . .

As he'd expected, Rose Cottage was in darkness. The storm was unabated, roaring furiously about his ears, with great streaks of energy exploding against the night sky. As he hammered on the front door his hair whipped about his face and water poured beneath the collar of his rain jacket.

Marissa, feeling her way gingerly to the kitchen to find the stub of candle she knew was there, froze in fear.

'Oh, s-stinging scorpions,' she squeaked.

Who would come visiting in the middle of a storm? And it was already nine o'clock. Her heart almost stopped at her next thought. Perhaps it was someone from the hospital, coming to say that grandfather was unwell again . . .

She stumbled to the front door and unlocked it, leaving the chain in place while she peeked through the gap.

'Wh-who is it?' Unfortunately that stutter was back.

'Jonathan Gray. Open up, Marissa, for pity's sake.'

Marissa could hardly hear him and was forced to yell above the noise of the rain.

'I'm about to go to bed. Wh-what do you want?'

Jonathan swallowed back a sharp word. 'I've come to see if you're all right.'

'Oh. Well I'm perfectly OK, thank you.' She shuddered. 'Except for the fright you gave me!'

'Are you going to let me in?' he shouted, 'it's wild outside.'

Hurriedly Marissa drew back the chain. 'Sorry. Do come in.'

Jonathan lost no time in complying, only to stand dripping all over her newly cleaned hall carpet. He shook the rain from his hair and glowered at her.

'Strewth, girl, what took you so long?'

'Calm down, there's no need to yell.'

'I'm not yelling. Well, maybe just a little.' He shrugged out of his jacket, hung it on the oak coat stand next to the door and raked his sopping hair.

'Now that I'm here, how about a cup of coffee?'

He hadn't meant to say that. He'd meant to say what he'd come for and scoot.

A flash of lightning lit the heavens once more, followed by one of the loudest thunderclaps Marissa had ever heard. She gave a squeal of pure fright as the living-room blazed with light.

Suddenly conscious of her flimsy night attire, she blushed rosily.

'Hang on . . . ' Hurriedly groping her way to the bedroom, she flung on a thick dressing gown. Hopefully it had been too dark for him to have noticed.

Jonathan had noticed all right. He

might be gifted with a vivid imagination but now wasn't the time to encourage it so he'd averted his eyes pretty pronto.

'I've brought you some candles,' he informed her, handing them over. 'The electricity won't be on again until tomorrow morning at the earliest. The on-call electricians will be out checking the power lines and I daresay one or two fallen trees have brought them down in places.'

'Thank you very much, Professor.'

Marissa's tones were cool as she tried to remain indifferent to his proximity. It was difficult to keep her emotions in order when every thud of her heart reminded her of what a hunk he was. It was a great pity he was getting married, or she would be very, very interested.

Once the candles were burning from their saucers she busied herself with the coffee mugs, silently commanding her hands to stop shaking.

'Are you cold?' Jonathan asked, watching her.

'No, why?'

'You're trembling.'

He subdued the sudden desire to fold her in his arms and warm her against his heart, but that would be unwise in the extreme. It would not do to become involved with someone he should be avoiding like the plague.

'Well,' Marissa explained reasonably, 'I've had a fright.'

Who was she kidding? She was trembling all over, brimming with adrenalin because of the effect Jonathan Gray had on her. It was the same feeling she received when she read a Brett Morgan novel, only this man was flesh and blood and she couldn't very well close the book and put him away, could she? At all costs she must try to appear cool and nonchalant.

Jonathan grinned. 'You're not used to these country storms, are you?'

'Well, no. Do you take milk and sugar?'

'Black, no sugar.'

He took the tray from her, noting that she'd produced a plate of chocolate chip cookies as well . . . which served to remind him of Jamie and the other reason he was here.

Back in the living-room he took a grateful sip of the steaming liquid and curled his still damp hands around the mug to warm them. The action kept him from reaching for her.

'Miss Boyd . . . blast! Must I keep calling you Miss Boyd? And I would rather you didn't address me as Professor all the time. The name's Jonathan.'

Marissa shrugged. 'OK. You may call me Marissa.'

'Well, Marissa, I have a particular request from Jamie. Would you be prepared to come up to the house tomorrow and teach him how to make er, egg cups? He appears to have an interest in egg cups at the moment. Heaven alone knows why.'

Marissa beamed. 'I'd be delighted. It would be a lot easier, though, if he came here to my studio. I'm a potter, you see.'

'Ah. A creative lady. I might have known. But unfortunately Jamie is in bed at the moment, recovering from a throat infection.'

Marissa put down her mug. 'Oh, the poor darling.' That explained why he hadn't been down to Rose Cottage again. She'd imagined it was because his uncle had forbidden him to do so.

'I thought you said I wasn't fit to have anything to do with your nephew,' Marissa couldn't resist reminding him sweetly.

Jonathan frowned. 'I must apologise for that.' How could he explain that he was scared out of his wits that he'd fall for her?

'You'll come, then?'

'Nothing would keep me away. He'll be feeling bored and in need of some mental stimulation, not to mention TLC. Someone needs to take an interest in the child — ' she clapped a hand over her mouth, 'I'm sorry, that sounded rude. I'm sure his mother takes every interest . . . '

Jonathan's expression had turned bleak. 'Quite.'

A moment later Marissa looked up to surprise something in his eyes which caused her heart to flip.

He smiled faintly. 'You really care about Jamie, don't you?'

'Yes. He's an endearing little boy and I wish . . . '

'You wish?'

She blushed. 'I wish he were mine.'

Jonathan swallowed the rest of his coffee in one gulp and sprang up. He looked all at once stern and remote.

'I must go,' he clipped. 'Goodbye, Miss Boyd.'

He grabbed his jacket and was gone before Marissa could blink.

★ ★ ★

The wind had dropped but it was still raining the following morning when Marissa removed a batch of chocolate brownies from the oven and placed them in a container, ready for their 'picnic'.

127

Into a basket she had also popped a colourful rug, two bottles of juice and a couple of hard boiled eggs together with paper, felt pens and a story book.

In the bedroom she pinned her glossy hair into an artful knot before applying a touch of lip gloss and mascara.

'I'll be back to give you your lunch, Tippy,' she told the cat. 'Take good care of those babies while I'm away.'

Tippy paused in the action of licking a kitten and tossed her a haughty look. She always took good care of her babies!

Marissa hurried to the garage for the clay she'd prepared and stored in an airtight container, and placed it in a carrier bag together with one or two other items of equipment and a piece of board. She intended to give Jamie a happy and productive morning.

Mrs Nibela, dusting the living-room, looked out of the window when she heard Marissa's car purr up the drive. She hurried to the front door with a beaming smile.

'You have come to see the professor again, Miss Boyd? That is good.'

He appeared to be frustrated this morning, having eaten his breakfast in a silence which she knew signalled as great unhappiness. He was angry for some reason, too. She always knew when he was angry because his face became set in a blank mask. Perhaps a visit from the lovely Miss Boyd would cheer him up.

'No, Mrs Nibela,' Marissa informed her, 'I have come to spend the morning with Jamie.'

Mrs Nibela hid her disappointment. 'I will take you upstairs, then, Miss. Come with me.'

Marissa followed her through the hall, a large, deeply carpeted area with gilt-framed portraits of previous Grays staring down at them from white-washed walls. A bowl of brilliant summer flowers graced an oak table and an antique long case clock was just striking the hour of ten.

Nerina, coming down the gracious

staircase looking like something out of a fashion magazine, stared at her in shock.

'What do you want?' she demanded loudly, suddenly looking as cross as two sticks. 'What are you doing here?'

Before Marissa could reply Nerina's expression changed to one of smug cunning. 'You've come to speak to me about the cottage, of course. Your grandfather has decided to come to his senses after all.' She descended the rest of the staircase and gestured curtly. 'Come into the small sitting-room and we will do our business in there.'

Marissa eyed her coldly. How on earth could a man like the professor have allowed himself to become entangled with someone like this? On second thoughts, the professor was as bad as she was. He and this shrew of a woman were trying to turn her grandfather out of his home. How could she have forgotten?

'I have not come to do business with you, Mrs Gray,' she said firmly, 'I've come to see Jamie.'

Nerina's mouth dropped open. 'Jamie? What has the wretched child got to do with the sale of Rose Cottage?'

She wasn't very bright, Marissa thought in sudden rage. And neither was her charming little son 'wretched'!

'Let me make myself clear, Mrs Gray. Rose Cottage is not for sale and never will be. Now if you'll excuse me . . . '

'You hussy,' shrilled Nerina. 'Go away at once!'

A door was flung open and Jonathan Gray looked at them expressionlessly.

'Something wrong, Nerina? I heard voices.'

Nerina's face underwent a remarkable transformation. It cracked into a hard, brilliant smile.

'Oh, hello, darling. Nothing's wrong. This young woman was just leaving. I was just seeing her to the door.'

Marissa had had enough of the odious woman. She said clearly, 'I'm not leaving, Mrs Gray. The professor asked me to come here today to entertain Jamie and that is what I intend to do.'

Nerina rounded on Jonathan. 'Is that true? You invited her here? Why?'

His face was inscrutable. He said pleasantly, 'I apologise for Mrs Gray's ungracious welcome, Miss Boyd. Thank you for coming. Mrs Nibela will take you upstairs now.'

Marissa, who had swallowed back an unwelcome surge of pleasure at the sight of him, now swallowed back anger. She was angry with him, angry with Mrs Gray and angry at herself. She had no business falling in love with this ruthless man despite the charm he could lay on when he so wished. Jamie or no Jamie, this was the last time she would ever set foot in Dargle Park!

She summoned a determined smile, thanked Mrs Nibela for showing her the way and knocked on Jamie's door.

Mrs Nibela returned to her dusting, her spirits greatly lifted. The young lady was no pushover. She'd put Mrs Gray firmly in her place. The professor should open his eyes . . .

'Hi, Miss Boyd,' Jamie greeted her, bounding out of bed. He gave her a great hug around the waist. 'I've been waiting hours and hours for you. Uncle Jonathan said you would be coming to teach me about the egg cups.'

Marissa smiled warmly. 'That was a lovely hug, Jamie. Yes, I've brought you a basket full of goodies and we'll have a great time. But first, let's have our picnic. It's time for morning tea and I'm starving.'

Jamie's eyes grew large as she spread her tartan rug on the carpet and invited him to sit down as she unpacked the supplies she'd brought.

'Boiled eggs!' he shouted, 'I love boiled eggs. And you've drawn faces on them!'

'We'll eat them later. I've brought them so we can get the size right for moulding the egg cups. We have to roll long strips of clay and then coil them round and round, you see, and then we make a little base to put the cup on.

After that I'll take them home and fire them in the kiln so they can harden.'

'What's in this box?'

'Chocolate brownies. And when we've had our picnic and made our egg cups we'll have a story about Ferdinand Frog who wanted to be a fireman. And if you like, we can draw the fire engine and cut it out. It would make a great picture for your wardrobe door, wouldn't it?'

'Can we do some fractions afterwards?' he asked eagerly. 'I'm beginning to like doing sums now.'

Marissa felt a little glow of satisfaction beneath her ribs.

'We can certainly do a few fractions. Old Bucky is going to be highly pleased with you when you go back to school . . . '

Jonathan, having had a terse word with Nerina in private, stared helplessly out of the study window. In his present frame of mind he was finding it extremely difficult to settle to his writing.

It was a damnable situation to be in.

He was in love with one woman whilst being forced into a loveless marriage with another. Even Brett Morgan would be hard put to extricate himself from a difficulty like this!

That he had fallen heavily for Marissa Boyd he now no longer bothered to deny. She was all he wanted in a woman, and the complete antithesis of Nerina Gray. However, he had given Nerina his word and he would not go back on it. For Jamie's sake he must go through with this marriage even though it was becoming more unpalatable by the day.

Unable to help himself he strode from the room, mounted the steps two at a time and fetched up outside Jamie's door just in time to hear a most interesting conversation. At any other time it would have filled him with jubilation. Right now it only served to depress him further.

# 6

'My mother won't allow me to put up any pictures, Miss Boyd. She says I'm not allowed.'

'Never mind, I'll take it with me and put it up in my studio. And when you bring pictures home from school at the end of term I'll put them up there, too. Would you like that?'

'Yes. I wish you were my mother, Miss Boyd. Will you be my secret mum? I don't really like my real mum.'

Marissa's eyes moistened. 'I'd be honoured, Jamie.'

He sighed. 'When she marries my uncle Jonathan next month she'll probably spend more time with me, but I don't really want that. She's weird.

'My dad,' he continued to explain, 'was Uncle Jonathan's brother, and now that my dad's dead she's going to marry my Uncle Jonathan. But I don't want him to marry her. I want him to marry you.'

'Out of the mouths of babes,' muttered Jonathan despairingly as he stood in the passage. About to turn away, his attention was riveted by Jamie's next question.

'Would you like to marry Uncle Jonathan, Miss Boyd?'

Marissa hesitated. 'That situation won't arise, Jamie.'

'I know, but would you?' he insisted.

'Well, to be completely honest . . . Yes, Jamie, I would if the circumstances were different. He's a very attractive man.' And the nearest thing to Brett Morgan she would ever find.

Unable to bear listening to another word, Jonathan turned away. He felt more wretched than ever.

★ ★ ★

Tom Boyd opened his eyes and blinked. The bespectacled stranger standing next to his bed was well dressed and businesslike.

'Good morning, Mr Boyd. My name is Jeremy Carter from Carter Estates in Howick. I'm sorry to disturb you, but I have here a document for your signature, if you would be so kind?'

He opened a briefcase and extracted a sheet of paper.

'A Mrs Nerina Gray of Dargle Park has informed me that you have agreed to sell her your cottage. I believe you have discussed the terms. Is that correct?'

Tom's eyes turned steely. 'No,' he said baldly.

The estate agent raised his eyebrows. 'Oh?' He glanced at the document in his hand and read out a figure. 'This figure is incorrect, then? Mrs Gray distinctly said — '

'Mrs Gray is lying, my good friend,' Tom snapped. 'I have no intention whatever of selling my home and I have already informed her of that decision. Kindly tell her not to bother me again!'

'But — '

'Good day to you, Mr Carter,' he told the bewildered man and closed his eyes again.

When Marissa arrived to see him that evening he told her all about it.

'That woman's becoming a darned nuisance. She tells me her fiancé wants the cottage back in the Dargle Park estate, and that she intends to give it to him as a wedding present. That's arrant poppycock!'

'What do you mean, Grandfather?'

'Jonathan Gray doesn't want the place at all. If he did, he'd have discussed it with me outright instead of getting that shrew to do it. I know Jonathan, Marissa, he's a honourable man and he certainly doesn't lack courage. He's no fool, either. We've become pretty close, the two of us. He looks on me as a father, you know.'

'If he's that intelligent, why on earth would he want to go and marry a woman like Nerina?'

'That,' declared her grandfather, 'is

what I'm trying to fathom out. There is something here which doesn't quite add up.'

'Well, I daresay it's none of our business.'

She kissed him on the cheek. 'I'll go now. See that you get better soon, Grandfather. It's lonely at Rose Cottage without you.'

He smiled. 'Oh, I intend to be home before you can wink, love. Take care of yourself, now.'

'I will.'

'And don't let that woman come anywhere near the cottage.'

'I don't think that's likely to happen. Everything will be fine, Grandfather.'

A false confidence, as it turned out.

On her return to the cottage, Marissa parked her car under the acacia tree as usual. She walked towards the front door, key in hand, thinking about the next day. She would go into her studio straight after breakfast and spend the whole morning there; making the items she hoped to sell to the tourists just before Christmas. After that she would glaze Jamie's egg cups . . .

Halfway along the path she looked up and froze. Something was wrong. The house was in darkness and she distinctly remembered having left a light on in the hall. Her eyes widened in horror as she saw the glass on the front path, the result of a newly shattered living-room window.

With a small cry she turned and ran back to the car. No way was she going back inside the cottage. There might be someone still in there, waiting for her! Without another thought she fired the engine and raced up the hill to Dargle Park. Jonathan would know what to do . . .

Mrs Nibela had gone to her small home in the grounds and Jonathan was in the kitchen, pouring himself another cup of coffee. Nerina had taken herself off somewhere and hadn't yet returned, and he was feeling unaccountably restless. When he heard the frantic hammering on the front door he set his mug down hurriedly and went to open it.

'Marissa!'

She looked as though she'd seen something dreadful. Someone had frightened the life out of her, that much was clear. The poor girl couldn't even speak.

He put an arm around her shoulders and ushered her inside. 'What's the problem, Marissa?'

'The cottage,' Marissa croaked. Her heart was hammering so hard she couldn't get the words out coherently. 'Someone . . . the window . . . '

He placed gentle hands on her shoulders. 'Take a deep breath . . . that's better. Now tell me.'

'Someone went to the cottage while I was visiting the hospital,' she gulped. 'They've broken the living-room window and I'm too afraid to go inside. Will you come?'

Jonathan uttered a sharp word under his breath. 'Of course.'

He bundled her back to the car and took the wheel himself. In two seconds flat they were back at the cottage.

'Stay here while I take a look,' he ordered. 'Lock yourself in.'

Marissa was only too happy to do as he suggested until she heard the sounds of a scuffle taking place in the living-room. Without further thought for her safety she ran into the hall and flung on the light.

Jonathan was standing over the prone figure of a man.

'Here's your culprit,' he said, breathing hard. 'He was waiting in the darkness. I'm afraid he won't be going anywhere in a hurry,' he added with satisfaction.

Marissa scarcely heard him. She was staring about her in horror. The place had been completely ransacked . . . cases smashed, cushions slashed and papers strewn all over the carpet. And that was only the start. Broken crockery littered the kitchen floor, the contents of the drawers had been overturned and of her beloved Tippy there was absolutely no sign.

'The babies,' she moaned, and ran to the cardboard box. They were there, snug and warm, peeping up at her sleepily.

Jonathan was speaking on the telephone while he kept an eye on the unconscious figure on the floor. Two officers from the constabulary in Howick arrived within minutes, inspected the cottage, and began to take statements.

The man on the floor gave a groan, sat up and looked about him sullenly.

'I've seen him before,' Jonathan told the policeman. 'He was at the airport the day I collected my fiancée. A Mr Marlin Conrad . . . '

'Thank you, sir.'

To Marlin Conrad he said firmly, 'Come with us, mister, you're under arrest . . . '

When they'd gone, Marissa burst into tears.

'Why would he do a thing like this?' she sniffed.

Jonathan looked grim. He had a few ideas of his own, but now wasn't the time to enlighten her.

Marissa swallowed back the tears. 'Tippy's gone . . . '

'She'll be in the garden somewhere, Marissa. Don't worry, she won't leave her kittens for long; she'll be back. It was the noise which frightened her.'

'I hope you're right.'

He placed one hand on her shoulder. 'I'm taking you back to Dargle Park now where you'll spend the night. There's nothing further you can do until tomorrow, when we'll organise some help in cleaning this lot up. You'll need a glazier to mend the window.'

Marissa nodded. 'All right. I'll just fetch my night things.'

Half-an-hour later she was tucked up in bed with a mug of cocoa in her hands. Her last thought before she fell into an exhausted sleep was that Jonathan had taken charge exactly as Brett Morgan would have done. She must remember to thank him in the morning . . .

Nerina, waiting in the lounge of The

Haven for Marlin's return, looked at her watch for the twentieth time in as many minutes. What was keeping him? It was a simple matter to trash a house, surely? She'd told him to leave the Boyd woman alone should she return before he'd finished, but perhaps he'd lost his head and overdone it. If that was the case, the fool could stew in his own juice!

By eleven o'clock when he'd still not returned she left him a huffy note and returned to her car. She wasn't his keeper, she reflected crossly. Marlin was big and ugly enough to take care of himself.

In the morning she appeared at the breakfast table dressed like a fashion plate and humming smugly under her breath. Hopefully the Boyd girl and her grandfather would now understand that she meant business! It wouldn't take much to get them to agree to a sale after this; they'd be too terrified to disagree. She just had to approach the matter in the right way. Marlin would be back at The Haven by now and she must remember to tell him off for making her wait so long last night . . .

'Good morning, darling,' she greeted Jonathan, and then stopped dead at the sight of Marissa who was calmly buttering a slice of toast.

'What . . . what is that girl doing here?'

Jonathan rose and greeted her smoothly. 'Good morning, Nerina. I invited Miss Boyd to stay overnight as there was an unfortunate incident at Rose Cottage last evening.' He was watching her intently. 'Do you know anything about it?'

Hiding her fury, Nerina gave a tinkling laugh. 'Me?' She poured herself a cup of coffee from the pot on the sideboard and sat down, darting Marissa a sly, malicious glance. 'Why should I know anything about it?'

'Because a friend of yours was involved.'

Nerina choked on her first sip. 'What? Who?'

'Marlin Conrad.'

She went quite pale beneath her careful make-up, but looked up defiantly. 'Who is Marlin Conrad?'

Jonathan gave her a long, steady look.

'Marlin Conrad,' he said clearly, 'is the man you are having an affair with, my dear.'

This time Nerina didn't bother to hide her shock.

'Oh, I know all about it,' Jonathan added blandly, 'I wasn't born yesterday. You forget that I had ample opportunity to observe the way in which you treated my brother. I know all the signs, Nerina, so I did a little investigating of my own.'

He reached for another slice of toast. 'The question is, what do you intend to do now that your lover is in custody?'

Nerina's mouth opened and closed like that of a dying mackerel.

'One more thing, my dear,' he warned pleasantly, 'I would advise you to lay off the Boyds. Tom will never sell that cottage in a month of Sundays so you can stop pestering him. He told me about it on the telephone last night. I have no idea why you are so keen to acquire the property but I've been blessed with a good imagination so allow me to guess: you and Conrad wish to set up some sort of illegal activity in an isolated place, the goal of which would be the acquisition of a certain amount of financial gain. Filthy lucre, I think they call it.'

Nerina's eyes widened. 'How . . . how did you know?'

'Oh, I have a friend who is a private investigator. It was Brett Morgan who first put me on to the idea. He's a first class detective, you know.'

'You pig!' she shrilled.

Unable to handle any more, Nerina flung down her table napkin and flounced from the room.

Marissa was staring at Jonathan as though he had two heads. He ignored the look and said blandly, 'I'm sorry you had to listen to all that, Marissa, but I think it is just as well that you know the facts. I doubt you will be troubled any further by my . . . ' his lips twisted, ' . . . errant fiancée.'

At that moment his errant fiancée was heard roaring down the drive in his silver Mercedes, grinding up the gravel as she went.

Jonathan winced. 'The tyres . . . '

'About Brett Morgan,' Marissa accused. 'You said you know him. You said he's a friend. That's impossible!'

'Why?'

'Brett Morgan is a fictional character.'

'Not in my book, he isn't.'

There was a steely finality in his tones which told Marissa that the subject was closed. She shot him an uncertain look from puzzled green eyes. Perhaps he was referring to a different Brett Morgan.

She rose from the table. 'Well, anyway, I must thank you for allowing me to stay here overnight, and for all your help. I'd like to go now, Jonathan, if that's OK? I can manage the clearing up on my own so there will be no need to organise any help. You'll be busy today, what with taking Jamie back to school and so on.'

'You're sure?'

'Perfectly.'

'In that case, I'll walk you to your car.'

When she'd departed down the drive he heaved a frustrated sigh.

'Well, Brett Morgan,' he groaned, 'where do we go from here . . . ?'

# 7

The first thing Marissa did was look in the cardboard box to see if Tippy was there. Her cat stopped fussing with the kittens and gazed back at her with reproachful green eyes.

'Yes, yes, I know, you have my deepest apologies, Tippy. It won't happen again.'

Gingerly she went from room to room to assess the extent of the damage. When she came to the kitchen, she gave a despairing sigh. It was no use trying to make herself a cup of tea until the mess had been cleared up, but first she must telephone a glazier.

New crockery would have to be purchased as soon as possible as there was hardly a plate intact. However, nothing could replace her grandmother's antique tea set which had been hauled from the display cabinet and smashed, along with the nineteenth century gilded goblet the old lady had treasured so much. Grandfather would be heartbroken.

Grimly Marissa set to work, determined not to allow herself to be beaten despite the many questions which were buzzing around in her head.

★   ★   ★

Marlin Conrad sat clicking his knuckles as he waited in the police cell. If that stupid fiancé of Nerina's hadn't arrived everything would have worked out just fine, he thought sourly. He'd have sorted out the girl in no time and Nerina would be signing for the property this very morning . . .

When he heard her heels clicking down the passage, he looked up hopefully. Nerina, accompanied by the officer on duty, greeted him with a thinly-veiled sneer.

'You're a right fool, aren't you, Marlin?' she mocked. 'But never mind,

I've come to bail you out.'

An hour later they were sitting in the lounge of The Haven, drinking copious cups of coffee.

'It wasn't my fault,' he whined. 'If that fiancé of yours hadn't interrupted things when he did — '

'Don't speak to me about Jonathan,' Nerina snapped. 'I'm finished with him. He's a jerk.'

Marlin smirked. 'I could have told you that long ago. Why, may I ask, have you changed your mind so suddenly?'

'He knows all about us and why we want Rose Cottage, and he'll never marry me now, much less allow me to make free with his money. He's not the fool I thought he was, Marlin. He's been having us watched by some private investigator by the name of Morgan.'

She sighed regretfully. 'We'll have to change our plans. Now you're known to the police in this area they'll be sniffing around night and day. We can't very well stay here, can we?'

Marlin swore roundly. 'I didn't think of that. You're right, we must change our plans.'

'You'll have to think of something quickly, then, Marlin, because I'm getting really fed up.'

A sly smile crept over his face. 'I know exactly what we will do.'

'What?'

'The stolen car thing is too tame, Marina. I'd like to try something more daring.'

She eyed him with renewed interest. 'Oh? What is that?'

'My uncle has a jewellery business in Amsterdam and he's been on at me to join him.' He winked at her. 'He's a sharp one, if you know what I mean?'

'Get to the point, Marlin.'

'Well, the point is. I have a few contacts in Botswana, know what I mean?'

Nerina looked blank. 'No. I don't.'

'Ever heard of IDB?'

Her gaze suddenly widened. 'You mean illicit diamond buying? Are you

155

saying you can get us some illegal diamonds from the mine in Botswana?'

'That's exactly what I'm saying. With the contacts I have I can get plenty, and quickly, too. I just have to look the guys up and flash around a bit of the paper stuff, know what I mean?'

'Where will you get the money?'

'We'll sell your ring, for a start. And I've still got something coming to me from that last lot of stolen cars. It'll take about a week . . . '

He glanced disdainfully at her left hand. 'Don't worry, baby, I'll give you a rock that'll make Jonathan's ring look like something out of a Christmas cracker. We'll get the diamonds and we'll dump them on my uncle and he'll know what to do with them. We'll make a fortune because he'll be only too happy to cut us in. In fact, it was my uncle who gave me the idea in the first place. I've been too busy with other things to do something about it, but now's the time.'

Marina laughed loudly. 'Darling,

you're a genius! We'll skip the country through those other contacts of yours and make for Europe!'

'Exactly.'

She ran a hand through her blonde curls and got up to preen in the large gilt mirror over the fire place.

'I'm particularly keen on France and Italy, Marlin. All those fashion houses, you know . . . '

Marlin slammed his coffee cup into its saucer. 'Come, Nerina, we have work to do. We must get out of here quickly.'

★   ★   ★

Jonathan drove Jamie back to school in the Land Rover reflecting that he would soon be forced to buy Nerina a car of her own because she was always taking the Mercedes just when he needed it.

To his relief Jamie had said nothing further about changing schools. As they negotiated the school drive he spotted one of his classmates and gave a confident wave.

'Goodbye, Uncle Jonathan.'

He ran up the front steps of the school eagerly enough, secure in the knowledge that old Bucky would be pleased with his homework.

Jonathan spent the rest of the morning with his solicitor in town and returned to Dargle Park where he found his housekeeper in a state of suppressed excitement.

'The Madam told me to give you this,' she informed him knowingly as she handed over a letter. 'The Madam has left Dargle Park and has taken all her things with her.'

Although she longed to inform him of the fact, it would not be appropriate to say that the Madam had had a gentleman friend with her.

'I see. Thank you, Mrs Nibela. Would you bring me a cup of coffee? I'll be in the study.'

With a sigh he sat down at his desk and slit open the envelope. Nerina would be informing him that she had gone back to Johannesburg for the time being, which suited him just fine. Life would return to normal for a few weeks and he would be able to finish his manuscript for the publisher. When the scheming woman returned just before Christmas she would be full of demands about the wedding and his life would never be the same again . . .

'Your coffee, Professor Gray,' Mrs Nibela clucked, placing a cup at his elbow. She scanned his face surreptitiously for any signs of unhappiness but the professor's expression was as bland as usual. Hopefully her employer would be a little happier now that Mrs Gray had left.

Jonathan's eyes were riveted on the words before him. As he read the blood began to zing in his veins.

*I am going to Botswana for a holiday,* Nerina had written. *When I return I shall be at my usual address in Johannesburg for two weeks. During that time I shall be available to sign any papers you require concerning the adoption of my son. After that I will be leaving the country and never wish to set eyes on either of you again . . .*

★　★　★

Tom Boyd was discharged from the hospital three weeks later, by which time Marissa had stocked the studio shelves with enough items to enable her to open her little shop for business. A freshly painted sign saying *Rose Cottage Pottery* hung from a wrought iron post at the front gate. Underneath in smaller letters were the words, *please ring for attention.*

Marissa accompanied her grandfather as they walked slowly around the garden admiring the summer annuals she had planted just after she'd arrived. The roses around the front door were looking much better, too, having been diligently fed and watered over the past weeks.

'You have certainly been working

hard, love,' her grandfather commented. 'Like me, the cottage has taken on a new lease of life despite that unfortunate incident last month.'

'The ransacking? Oh, I've put all that behind me,' Marissa declared stoutly. 'I decided to drop the charges against that man, you know. He has since disappeared and I really don't think he will trouble us again.'

She bent over to pluck the dead daisy head from its bush and added, 'Besides, we have the insurance money which has helped a lot. And it's nice to have some new things.'

'Yes.'

'I met Mrs Nibela at the supermarket in Howick and she told me that Nerina Gray went back to Johannesburg a few weeks ago. I daresay she'll be returning to Dargle Park soon, in time for her wedding to Jonathan.'

'When is that to be?'

Marissa ignored the sudden pain she felt somewhere in the region of her heart. The pain had been surfacing a lot of late, especially when she allowed her thoughts to dwell on a certain blue-eyed professor whose kiss she still treasured.

She said brightly, 'As far as I remember it will take place just before Christmas.'

'I can't think what he sees in that woman,' her grandfather growled. 'To think she actually tried to force us out of our home! It's a disgrace. I never imagined Jonathan had had anything to do with it, and I was right. He's an honourable man.'

'Yes. But we must put all Nerina's nonsense behind us and try to get on as good neighbours, Grandfather, because we'll have them on our doorstep for a long time to come. Besides, you wouldn't want to drop your friendship with Jonathan.'

'That is true. When is young Jamie coming home from school?'

'Tomorrow, I believe. He's bound to visit me soon because he'll want to make more egg cups, and I've promised him one of the kittens.'

Hurriedly she changed the subject. 'I put that business advertisement in the newspaper today.'

'You did?'

'Yes. I'm expecting to do some brisk trade when the tourists start descending. Apparently most of the craft shops and restaurants along the Midlands Meander are expecting a good turnout, what with it being the start of the December holidays.'

'Well, I'm sure things will go well. Remember, I shall be here to help you, love. I'll sit at the table and count all the money.'

She grinned. 'I'll hold you to that.'

★ ★ ★

Jonathan put down the telephone and punched the air in jubilation. His publisher had just informed him that the first edition was now available.

'Yes!' he grinned. 'Another Brett Morgan novel will be on the shelves in

163

time for Christmas.'

Due to unprecedented public demand the printing had been rushed through successfully. Not that it hadn't been a real sweat. It was as a result of Nerina's surprising letter that he'd suddenly taken on new energy and enthusiasm and been able to complete the manuscript weeks before time, which had pleased his publisher greatly.

Now he could begin to put his mind to other things. Christmas would soon be upon them and he must decide on a suitable gift for Jamie. He already knew what he would give the delightful Miss Boyd who had not ceased to occupy his thoughts constantly over the past weeks.

They had been busy for weeks, what with finishing the manuscript and rushing off to make two trips to Johannesburg to finalise matters concerning his adoption of Jamie. Of Nerina he had seen very little, but had heard from one of her cronies that she had already gone abroad. As far as he was concerned it was a happy solution all round. Jamie was now legally his son and he was at long last a free man.

Free, he reflected with deep content, to choose his own wife.

Jamie was waiting for him on the school steps with his luggage. He gave a smiling wave when he recognised the car.

'Hello, Uncle Jonathan, I can't wait to show you my book prize. I got it in Assembly this morning and Old Bucky gave it to me because my work has improved a lot and I like doing sums now.'

Jonathan ruffled his nephew's hair. 'Well done, Jamie. I'm proud of you.'

'Are we going to McDonald's for lunch again?'

'If that's what you'd like.'

'Well, if you don't mind I'd rather go straight home because Miss Boyd is going to give me one of Tippy's kittens. She writes to me every week, you know, and she says the kittens are big enough to leave their mother now. In fact, she says I can even have both kittens if you'll allow me. That way,' he told his uncle earnestly, 'they won't be lonely, will they? I mean, they'll have each other to play with when I go back to school again.'

'That's true,' Jonathan agreed gravely.

'Can I have them both, then?'

'Certainly.'

Jamie gave a great sigh of relief. 'Thank you, Uncle Jonathan.'

Jonathan glanced at the child's happy face and smiled.

'Jamie,' he said carefully, 'how would you like to start calling me Dad instead of Uncle? I know I can never replace your real father, but I'll have a jolly good try. You see old man, I have legally adopted you and according to the courts you are now actually my son.'

Jamie did not hesitate. 'Cool,' he nodded, adding with a grin, ' . . . Dad.'

'I have another piece of news for you. There will be no wedding this Christmas because your mother has decided not to marry me after all. In fact, she has gone to live overseas.'

Jamie's smile widened. 'That's cool, too.'

'You don't mind not seeing her for some time?'

Jamie shook his head. 'I won't need to see my mother if Miss Boyd's around.'

And that, thought Jonathan, said it all!

★ ★ ★

If Marissa's shelves were somewhat depleted by the end of the following week, her bank balance reflected a healthy increase. Two days before Christmas she drove into Howick where she collected the post and did some last-minute shopping.

It was good to be able to spend without too much restraint this year because she intended to make it one of the best Christmases her grandfather had ever had.

He had a cup of tea waiting as she parked the car under the acacia tree and carried her parcels into the house.

'There's lots of post today,' she told him as they sipped their tea, 'mainly Christmas cards, I should think.'

She ripped open an envelope addressed to them both in bold, masculine handwriting and discovered that it was not a Christmas greeting but an invitation.

'We are invited to a party at Dargle Park on Christmas eve, Grandfather.'

The old man seemed pleased. 'That is very kind of the Grays.'

'It will mean having to make polite conversation with Nerina,' she reminded him warily. 'I haven't wanted to ask Jamie, but I should imagine the wedding would have taken place by now.' And the mistress of the house would doubtless be queening it around the place, making everyone else unhappy. It was amazing how some people just had that ability.

'That need not bother us, love. It was you who said we must try to be good neighbours.'

What her grandfather didn't know was that the evening would be an excruciating ordeal for her. The thought of seeing Jonathan again and knowing she could never mean anything to him because he was in love with that awful woman caused her more pain that she cared to admit.

She'd been amazed to find that Jonathan Gray had come to mean more to her than even Brett Morgan, her secret hero. For appearances sake she would have to make the effort and go to the party because her grandfather had very few pleasures left to him and would enjoy having a chat with his old friend.

On the morning of the party Marissa paid a visit to one of the boutiques in Pietermaritzburg, determined to find a suitable dress. Nerina, of course, would look stunning and she had no intention of giving the woman an opportunity to sneer at her outfit.

Having found what she wanted, a silky, rose-pink designer creation with matching high heeled sandals, she didn't look twice at the cost. For once she would treat herself, and sought out a hairdresser who shampooed her hair and trimmed the ends so it fell in glossy layers about her bare shoulders.

'Very nice,' her grandfather commented as she snatched up a soft mohair wrap. It was a warm night but there was a hint of rain in the air.

'You look very nice, yourself.' Marissa smiled.

'Thank you, my dear. I'm looking forward to this. I haven't been to a party in years.'

They drove up the hill and parked on the drive of Dargle Park, surprised to find there were not as many cars as they'd expected.

'Perhaps it's not a very big party,' Marissa murmured.

Mrs Nibela ushered them inside, resplendent in a brightly-coloured dress and headscarf. She took Marissa's wrap and invited, 'Come into the living-room, Miss Boyd, Mister Boyd. The family is waiting for you.'

'Family?' Marissa gave her a puzzled glance.

'The professor's mother and father are here, and his sisters and their husbands, and of course, Master Jamie. They have a family party every Christmas, but this is the first time other people have been invited.'

A sudden interested silence fell as they entered the room. Marissa had the feeling that every eye was upon her in friendly assessment, and went faintly pink. When she encountered Jonathan's eyes across the room, the pink deepened. As a married man he should not be looking at her like that!

With a charming smile Jonathan detached himself and shook her grandfather by the hand.

'Tom . . . it's good to see you looking so well,' he told his friend warmly. He turned to Marissa with a polite nod. 'Marissa.'

'Good evening, Professor,' she replied

formally, not seeing the spark of laughter in his eyes.

'The name is Jonathan, remember? May I say that you're looking very lovely tonight? Come and be introduced . . . my family can't wait to meet you. You know Jamie, of course . . . '

Jamie, almost unrecognisably clean and tidy and wearing his new trainers, flung himself at Marissa with an enthusiastic hug.

'I'm so glad you could come, Miss Boyd. Agnes has made lots and lots of can . . . can . . . '

'Canapés.' She smiled. 'How are the kittens doing?'

'Oh, they're cool. Dad says they're the cutest things he's ever seen.'

'Your mother doesn't object to them, then?'

He looked blank. 'My mother? She's not here.' He added with childish candour, 'She's gone to live overseas. She won't be coming back here and she won't be marrying my dad any more.'

A rush of emotion, hastily concealed, brimmed over in Marissa's eyes. Jonathan was watching her intently, his face inscrutable. Being an observant man he had noted the mixture of hope and delight and it set his heart rate soaring. It was the very reaction he'd been hoping for.

When the introductions had been made Marissa accepted a glass of sherry and allowed herself to be drawn into conversation with Jonathan's sisters, all beautifully dressed and generous in their praise of her outfit.

By the end of the evening she had to admit that this family was delightful. Being an only child herself, she'd had no idea that siblings could be such fun. They were all decent, sincere people, happily married and devoted to their children. His elderly parents in particular had much in common with her grandfather, sharing the same sense of humour. Judging by their animated conversation and the laughter which accompanied it, her grandfather appeared to have enjoyed himself enormously.

'A happy evening.' He yawned when Marissa took him a last cup of tea in bed. 'Goodnight, my dear. Sleep well.'

Useless advice, as it turned out. She lay in bed until the dawn chorus sounded in the acacia trees outside her window. Her heart was singing because Jonathan wasn't going to marry Nerina after all, and at the car he'd kissed her goodnight in a most satisfying manner . . .

The incredible fact was that her secret hero, Brett Morgan, was fading more and more into the distance and a new hero was replacing him; a far more satisfactory and exciting man of flesh and blood.

As she watched the dawn light steel through the curtains Marissa asked herself the question which had begun to nag at her: did Jonathan feel the same way about her?

# 8

On Christmas morning Marissa drove her grandfather in to St Luke's Church for the service after which they opened their presents and ate a sumptuous dinner.

'Dear, dear,' her grandfather muttered happily, 'I shall have to go and take a nap. You don't mind, Marissa?'

'Not at all, Grandfather. I'll bring you a cup of tea later on.'

'What a treasure you are.' He yawned sleepily and went to his bedroom.

Marissa tidied the kitchen and had just taken herself outside to sit in the sun on the patio when she looked up in surprise.

'Merry Christmas, Marissa.'

Jonathan placed two gaily wrapped gifts on the table. 'I hope I'm not disturbing you?'

His gaze was intent as he looked

down at her, half smiling.

Marissa's breath locked in her throat.

'N-not at all,' she managed politely. He was looking as magnificent as ever in a pair of well-fitting denim jeans and a casual shirt which made his eyes seen more intensely blue.

'Th-these are for us? How kind. Thank you.'

He grinned, 'The whisky's for your grandfather.'

'Naturally. And this one's for me . . . a book?' She looked up. 'I love reading.'

She tore off the wrapping and gasped.

'Oh! It's the latest Brett Morgan novel!' Her green eyes shone. 'I had no idea that another one was just out. This is absolutely marvellous.'

Spontaneously she jumped up and kissed him on the cheek. 'Grandfather will have to get his own supper tonight because I'll be reading into the small hours.'

Unable to wait another second, she opened the title page and then gasped.

An inscription had been written in Jonathan's bold scrawl.

*To Marissa Boyd, friend, admirer and loyal champion of Brett Morgan — not to mention erstwhile fiancée — this comes with my best wishes.*

She laughed. 'Thank you, Jonathan. And now, I can't resist taking a peek at the first sentence . . . '

Hastily she flicked over the pages to chapter one.

*The city seemed more grey than usual. Brett Morgan pulled up the collar of his well-worn navy overcoat and stepped out into the icy drizzle . . .*

Marissa stopped and frowned. 'I wish Brett would buy himself another raincoat. I don't like navy, it's so dull.'

Jonathan's mouth twitched. 'I'll tell him.'

'Don't be daft, he's a fictional character.'

'So he is. I'll leave you in peace, then, Marissa. Enjoy your time with Brett.'

He was gone before she could draw breath.

With a great, happy sigh Marissa settled down to read.

It was the following afternoon that she finally reached the last chapter of the novel. After reading the final, satisfying sentence she sighed again and then idly turned the page. To her amazement Jonathan's scrawl appeared once more, the words starkly written in black ink. They had her eyes popping from their sockets.

*Marissa, I love you dearly. Will you marry me? I know I'm not a patch on Brett Morgan but I'll do my best.*

It was signed by the author, DJ Grayson.

Marissa jumped to her feet in shock.

'DJ Grayson,' she murmured incredulously, ' . . . is Jonathan Gray!'

Happy tears spilled from her green eyes. She flung down the book, raced up the hill to Dargle Park and fetched up panting and breathless on the front veranda where she leaned on the doorbell.

Jonathan, who had been prowling

impatiently at the window of his study all morning, nervously raked his hair. He forced himself to wait as Mrs Nibela answered Marissa's summons.

'The professor . . . is he in? I must see him at once!' Her eyes shone and her cheeks were pink more from the force of her emotions than the race up the hill.

Mrs Nibela took one look and chuckled. 'Of course he is in. He has been waiting for you.' She knew that because her employer had been like a cat on bricks, unable to settle to anything all morning.

'Miss Boyd to see you, sir,' she announced smugly before withdrawing to the kitchen to inform Agnes that they must be prepared for a special celebration because she, Rose Nibela, could feel it in her bones.

Marissa waited until the door was closed.

'The answer,' she gabbled, still breathless from her exertions, 'is yes, yes, yes, I will, but why didn't you tell me who you were? Actually to be honest you've been my secret hero for weeks now and I don't mind in the least that you're not him and I thought you were going to marry that woman and I was so unhappy until I found out you weren't and now I'm not in love with him any more . . . '

Jonathan had no difficulty whatever in interpreting this garbled utterance. He opened his arms wide and Marissa, with a happy sigh, ran into them.

'I'm glad too,' he told her in a gruff voice. 'I've been on the point of asking you to marry me so many times but I wasn't sure how you'd react once you knew I was DJ Grayson and Brett's creator.' He grinned. 'The competition's been pretty stiff.'

Marissa laughed. 'Not any more. I'm consigning Brett to the pages, where he belongs.'

'I'm relieved to hear it. How soon can we be married, Marissa?'

She pretended to think. 'Well, I'll have to consult with Mrs Tippet.'

'Who?'

'Tippy. She might not wish to live at Dargle Park with those two naughty kittens under her feet all day.'

'In that case she can stay at Rose Cottage and keep your grandfather company. We wouldn't want him to be too lonely.'

'Oh, Grandfather will be delighted with our news. I'll be seeing him often, anyway, when I go down to my studio. I'll need to keep my hand in, you know, and I've been considering giving a few pottery lessons.'

'Whatever makes you happy,' Jonathan told her. 'And now, my darling, I intend to kiss you, and I can promise that I'll make a better job of it than Brett Morgan.'

Which he did.

'Let's go and find Jamie, shall we?' he suggested when he'd made his point to Marissa's complete satisfaction.

' . . . After all, he'll want to know how soon he can start calling you 'Mum'!'

We do hope that you have enjoyed reading this large print book.

Did you know that all of our titles are available for purchase?

We publish a wide range of high quality large print books including:
**Romances, Mysteries, Classics**
**General Fiction**
**Non Fiction and Westerns**

Special interest titles available in large print are:
**The Little Oxford Dictionary**
**Music Book, Song Book**
**Hymn Book, Service Book**

Also available from us courtesy of Oxford University Press:
**Young Readers' Dictionary**
**(large print edition)**
**Young Readers' Thesaurus**
**(large print edition)**

For further information or a free brochure, please contact us at:
**Ulverscroft Large Print Books Ltd.,**
**The Green, Bradgate Road, Anstey,**
**Leicester, LE7 7FU, England.**
**Tel:** (00 44) **0116 236 4325**
**Fax:** (00 44) **0116 234 0205**

# AZETTE FROM JERSEY

## Irene Castle

When Azette flew from Jersey to the West Country, to find her favourite cousin Dennis, she also made new friends: Jane, now her flat-mate, and Mandy, who refuses to name her baby's father and needs help. At Jane's family home Azette is introduced to Andrew, a handsome — if moody — farmer . . . She is reunited with her cousin Dennis, but suddenly their relationship changes, and their plans to return to Jersey together crumble. Now Azette has a difficult decision to make . . .

# THE STOLEN IMAGE

## Elaine Daniel

Alexei Baran is the notoriously difficult, publicity-shy star of the Imperial Ballet. On the strength of her previous pictures of him Anna, a photographer, is asked to portray the ballet company at work. Almost in self-defence she becomes engaged to James Farmer, but this proves to be no protection at all against falling in love with Baran. But when he discovers how she has used his captured image, Alexei is determined that she should steal no more of him . . .

# A KISS IN TANGIER

## Denise Conway

Flying to Tangier to look after five-year-old Tommy is more complicated than Eve had expected: Dean, a widower, is an indifferent father, and his Arab housekeeper sinister. Puzzled and uneasy, Eve turns to Evan, a young man who assisted her before. However, when Nadia arrives Eve realises that her new-found love is doomed, although she is too entangled in the web of intrigue to leave. And when danger threatens, her only thought is to help the man she loves.

*By Alice Raine*